'If anyone can do it, it will be you and your *Edelweiss*. For you are . . . *my eagles in*

## Also by Leo Kessler

The *SS Assault Regiment Wotan* Series
SS PANZER BATTALION
DEATH'S HEAD
CLAWS OF STEEL
GUNS AT CASSINO
THE DEVIL'S SHIELD
HAMMER OF THE GODS
FORCED MARCH
BLOOD AND ICE
THE SAND PANTHERS
COUNTER-ATTACK
PANZER HUNT
SLAUGHTER GROUND
HELLFIRE
FLASHPOINT
CAULDRON OF BLOOD
SCHIRMER'S HEADHUNTERS
WHORES OF WAR
SCHIRMER'S DEATH LEGION

The *Stormtroop* Series
STORMTROOP
BLOOD MOUNTAIN
VALLEY OF THE ASSASSINS
RED ASSAULT
HIMMLER'S GOLD
FIRE OVER KABUL
WAVE OF TERROR

The *Otto Stahl* Series
OTTO'S PHONEY WAR
OTTO'S BLITZKRIEG!
OTTO AND THE REDS

The *Sea Wolves* Series
SINK THE SCHARNHORST!
DEATH TO THE DEUTSCHLAND

Also:

As Klaus Konrad
The *Russian* Series
FIRST BLOOD
MARCH ON MOSCOW
FRONT SWINE

Leo Kessler

# Eagles in the Snow

*Stormtroop 8*

Futura
Macdonald & Co
London & Sydney

A Futura Book

First published in Great Britain in 1983
by Futura Publications, a Division of
Macdonald & Co (Publishers) Ltd
London & Sydney



ISBN 0 7088 2355 6

Filmset, printed and bound in Great Britain by
Hazell Watson & Viney Ltd, Aylesbury, Bucks

Futura Publications
A Division of
Macdonald & Co (Publishers) Ltd
Maxwell House
74 Worship Street
London EC2A 2EN

# *A CALL TO ARMS*

'Man, in the battle of our days, is a man, who hardly knowing how to swim, is suddenly thrown into the sea.'

*Ardant du Picq*

*'HEAVEN, ARSE, CLOUDBURST . . . WE'VE GOT HIM . . . WE'VE GOT THE TOMMY BASTARD . . . RIGHT IN THE GUTS . . . WE'VE GOT HIM! . . .'*

The haggard, unshaven mountain troopers grouped around the chattering machine gun, sending angry red tracer streaming in a hasty curve into the hard, blue northern sky, sprang up and down excitedly, slapping each other on the back, faces wild with triumph.

'Cease fire . . . In three devils' name, *cease fire*!' *Leutnant* Ferdl barked above the racket, still keeping the stricken plane inside the gleaming calibrated circles of glass as he followed its descent with his glasses.

His gunners, tucked away on the craggy plateau overlooking the harbour, had hit the Tommy plane all right. There was no doubt about that. Thick, evil-black smoke was streaming from the Anson's port engine and the other engine was giving off a series of throaty coughs, as if it might pack up at any moment. He could well imagine the Tommy pilot up there, his face crimson and lathered with hot sweat, fighting desperately, screaming with rage as he tried to keep the plane in the air.

But that wasn't to be. As the chatter of his machine guns died away, leaving behind a loud echoing silence filled only with the last dying splutters of the Anson's remaining engine, it, too, died.

The sudden silence and the abrupt realization that, up there, men were struggling for their lives overwhelmed the tough, hardy Bavarian mountain troopers. They stared at the stricken plane as it dropped lower and lower, coming ever closer to its inevitable doom, thick black smoke, from both engines now, streaming behind it in a pall of death.

*Leutnant* Ferdl tensed, the bright white knuckles of his hands clutching the binoculars. The Anson was heading straight for the peak directly ahead of them. All around him his men held their breaths. In an instant the Tommy would smash into the snow-covered rock and disintegrate.

At the very last moment the unknown pilot dragged up the plane's nose and it seemed to miss the peak by a matter of metres. Around the handsome young officer, the men breathed a collective sigh of relief and *Feldwebel* Muessli, whose machine gun had shattered the Anson's engines, gasped, 'Great crap on the Christmas tree – now I've gone and pissed myself!'

Nobody laughed. The situation was too tense.

Suddenly the unknown pilot spotted the high plateau before them, overlooking the icy-green waters of the fiord below. Somehow or other he forced the stricken plane round and came gliding in, undercarriage creaking down painfully.

*Leutnant* Ferdl remembered his military duties. What was this lone Tommy plane doing this far north on the second day of the invasion of Norway? Was it simply a reconnaissance plane – or something else? A great boost of adrenaline slammed into his bloodstream, and he forgot he had not had any sleep for forty-eight hours now, ever since General Dietl had alerted his pain-racked, sea-sick mountain troopers for the great assault landing on Narvik. 'Stand by to rescue the Tommy crew!' he barked.

'All right, you bunch of wet-tails,' *Feldwebel* Muessli echoed in a bellow that echoed and re-echoed in the arena of mountains all around them, 'you heard the officer. Stand by to rescue the buck-teethed T . . .' He stopped short. The Anson had fallen abruptly, as if the pilot had suddenly lost all control. '*Holy strawsack*,' he gasped. 'They're for the chop, now!'

The Anson hit the rock with a thunderous crash. Her undercarriage collapsed immediately. Her nose dipped. Both props bent like matchsticks. The plane ripped across the surface of the plateau at a hundred kilometres an hour, throwing up a wild wake of pebbles and dust, as the pilot fought to keep her from overturning. By some miracle he steered the plane between two huge boulders. Metal fell in a thick rain behind the Anson. Even at that distance *Leutnant* Ferdl could hear the terrible rending, screeching sound, as the rock ripped the guts out of the British machine. He gritted his teeth; the noise was almost unbearable. Ahead loomed the edge of the plateau. Below was a sheer drop of five hundred metres straight into the fiord. Ferdl's hands gripping his binoculars, as he followed the wild, final, bucking progress of the stricken plane, were soaked with sweat. The pilot couldn't make it. It was impossible. In a moment he'd zoom over the top to crash, broken to bits, into the bottomless depths below. At the very last instant, the plane, ploughing its way across the rock, veered to the left. Its left wing fell off like a great metal leaf, as it swung round in a crazy half circle. It exploded the next moment. Savage scarlet flame shot into the sky, as the Anson came to a rest at last, spinning on the very edge of the precipice. No one got out . . .

There was no sound now, save for the steady crackle of the burning engine and the howl of the icy wind which came down straight from the Arctic.

*Leutnant* Ferdl, his chest heaving with the effort on the hasty climb up to the plateau, swallowed hard. The pilot peered at him through the shattered spider's web of plexiglass, the control column thrust through his chest and pinning him to his seat, his face looking as if someone had just thrown a handful of strawberry jam at it. Behind him a man retched and vomited, seized by a sudden rush of nausea.

But there was more and worse to come. As they forced their way into the buckled, shattered interior littered with the broken chaos of that last flight – oxygen cylinders, seats, maps, bits of uniform – they came across the radio operator, or what was left of him. His head, complete with leather helmet and earphones and still attached by wires to the radio, swinging back and forth like some hideous child's toy, designed by a sadistic monster. Brushing aside an open-mouthed, gawping *Feldwebel* Muessli, *Leutnant* Ferdl stumbled outside, and with one hand pressed against the fuselage, he let the hot vomit flood his throat and drench the ground at his feet.

It was then that he saw the severed leg, still clad in the thick, fur-lined flying boot, and the trail of blood which led away from the shattered plane, a bright scarlet on the patches of snow – like juice freshly pressed from an over-ripe fig.

For a moment he could not understand. He stared at the trail, eyes blank of everything but tears from the retching; no comprehension. Then he had it, after what seemed an age. He straightened up and wiped the vomit from his bearded chin. '*Feldwebel*,' he said thickly, '*Fedelwebel* Muessli.'

'Sir!' Even Muessli, the former butcher from Munich, not particularly known for his sensitivity, was subdued after what he had seen in the plane. He took in the severed leg and then looked at the ashen-faced officer with the dribbles of vomit hanging from the black stubble of his chin.

Ferdl fought back bitter bile. 'Sergeant, somebody got out . . . the leg . . . and that trail of blood . . . leading to the rocks over there . . .'

Muessli silently nodded his big Bavarian head and began to unsling his short mountain carbine. He indicated to left and right. The troopers did the same. Unslinging their weapons, they stalked forward, coming in on both flanks, bodies crouched instinctively, as if they expected trouble at any moment.

*Leutnant* Ferdl pulled himself together. An officer should always be an example to his men, even though this was his first time in action. He drew his pistol, and forcing himself to walk erect, he advanced between the two files of cautious troopers. When he was some ten metres from the boulders, the trail of blood leading to them clearly visible now, he halted and cleared his throat, frantically trying to remember his schoolboy English from the days when he had taken his *abitur*[1] in what now seemed another age. 'Englishman,' he said with more confidence than he felt, 'you have no chance. Please surrender.' His voice almost broke; what he had seen these last minutes was really too much for him, '*Please!*'

His answer was a faint groan.

*Leutnant* Ferdl flung a glance at Muessli.

The latter nodded, his big broad butcher's face set hard. In the heavy silence that followed the groan, the sound of Muessli pulling back the bolt of his carbine made Ferdl jump. He swallowed hard and with a hand that trembled badly, for there was something eerie, uncanny about this whole thing – indeed the small blond hairs at the back of his head were standing erect with apprehension – he gave Muessli the infantry signal for Advance. Together the NCO and officer stalked forward, coming in on both sides of the boulder from behind which they had heard the groan.

Then they saw him, a tall fair man in the khaki of the British Army. His hair was matted with blood and oil, his face contorted with an agonized grimace of absolutely unbearable pain. There was a great red gaping hole where his right leg should have been, the bone glittering a brilliant white and the blood jetting in a scarlet stream with every heartbeat.

Ferdl gulped and nearly dropped his pistol.

It was a fatal move. The dying Englishman brought up the revolver he had concealed beneath the bloodstained briefcase, chained to his left wrist.

Ferdl screamed shrilly as the slug slammed into his belly. At that range the impact was so great that he was lifted clean off his feet and slapped against the boulder

[1] German high school leaving certificate.

behind him. He sprawled there dead, arms flung out as if crucified.

Slowly, infinitely slowly, eyelids flickering as if he were about to fall asleep at any moment, the dying Englishman turned the pistol in a wavering hand on an open-mouthed *Feldwebel* Muessli.

For what seemed an age the big ex-butcher simply stood there, watching the soldier, as if he was sitting at the movies, as if the scene had nothing to do with him. Then he saw the Englishman's knuckles whiten as he took the final pressure. In a second he'd fire. The spell broke. 'Why, you murdering bastard!' he screamed, voice suddenly high and hysterical like that of a woman.

He sprang forward, carbine upraised. For one fleeting moment he towered above the Englishman sprawled against the rock. Next moment, as if he were back in the Munich abbattoir stunning some great old sow with a hammer, he brought the cruelly shod butt of his carbine down on the Englishman's skull. It splintered like rotten wood. Gleaming white bone fragments flew everywhere and he jumped back hurriedly as a slurry of bright red blood flashed upwards. With the blood streaming from his nostrils and ears, the Englishman's shattered head slumped to his chest. He had been killed instantly by that tremendous blow.

Abruptly, the rage vanished from the big soldier's body, as if a tap had been suddenly opened. He looked from the man he had just killed, to *Leutnant* Ferdl, whose sightless eyes stared into infinity, then back to the Englishman. What was he to do? *Feldwebel* Muessli was not a man to act without orders. But now there was no one left to give him a command.

It was just at that moment that the first ammunition started to explode within the crashed plane, white and red tracer bullets zig-zagging crazily into the sky like a mad fireworks' display, and behind him the mountain troopers began to cry in alarm, '*Let's get out of here . . .*

*There's gas escaped everywhere . . . The whole shitting thing's gonna go up in the air in a minute . . .!'*

In a flash *Felbwebel* Muessli became aware of his own danger. But he couldn't just leave. How would he report to General Dietl if he was asked what had happened here on this high, wind-blown plateau? How would he explain *Leutnant* Ferdl's death? He wasn't an educated man; he had no gift for words. He'd make a fool of himself.

His eye fell on the briefcase chained to the Tommy's wrist. Of course, that would explain everything. The Tommy was an officer, he could see that from the stars on his blood-soaked tunic. He'd be carrying documents. That would tell the 'Old Man' everything he wanted; he would be spared the embarrassment of trying to explain in his usual, blundering tongue-tied manner.

He grabbed the chain, trying not to look at the dead man's shattered skull, and pulled. Nothing happened. From behind the rock, he could hear the first hush of exploding petrol. His back was suddenly struck by a wave of almost unbearable heat. The plane was beginning to burn. He hesitated no longer and dropped his gory carbine and whipped out his razor-sharp bayonet. He slashed it down hard on the man's wrist, above the chain. He heard the bone snap. His shoulder muscles flexing brutally, he repeated the stroke. The blade went clean through the rest of the bone. Another slash and the remaining skin was severed. The wrist, with the briefcase attached to it, fell to the rock. Muessli swallowed hard and grabbed it.

Next moment he was fleeing down the hillside with the rest, his face a livid red in the reflected light of the fiercely burning plane, as if the devil himself were after him . . .

# *BOOK ONE: CRASH LANDING*

# ONE

'All right, you bunch of wet-sacks, hark here!' Sergeant-Major Meier's tremendous voice echoed and re-echoed across the snowbound valley. Above the waiting *Edelweiss* troopers' heads, the mountain eagles rose in hoarse cawing protest at the noise.

Meier, known as Ox-Jo to the men of Germany's elite mountain assault force *Stormtroop Edelweiss*, spread his legs and placed his big red hams of fists on his hips contemptuously. 'Now anyone who wants to risk a fat lip, better step forward now, 'cos I'm not gonna play wet-nurse this afternoon with you lot of asparagus Tarzans! From the goodness of my heart, I've been powdering your soft arses too long. Now it's got to end!'

From the rear rank, Jap blew the huge, red-faced sergeant-major a wet kiss and simpered in a shrill falsetto, 'But we still love you, Sarnt-Major, all the same.'

The tough mountain troopers, every one of them born in the mountains, laughed at the crack.

Colonel Stuermer, the elite Stormtroop's CO laughed with them, his blue eyes set in a handsome bronzed face sparkling in delight. Ox-Jo, the rogue, was in his usual good form. But then they all were, his men privileged to wear the treasured silver '*Edelweiss*'[1] badge at the side of their ski caps. They were at the peak of their form, every one of them brought up on skis, almost before they could walk, a match for many a professional climber, as well.

Stuermer's smile vanished, as he remembered yet again just what his Bavarian and Austrian youngsters were

[1] The mountain flower which grows only in the high mountains and which young Bavarian and Austrian boys, risking their necks to do so, pick for their girlfriends.

being trained for – another one of the Führer's crazy ventures which brought the Third Reich more glory, but only spelt misery for the poor soldiers who had to carry them out. He sighed and, telling himself that all had been peaceful since the German invasion of Poland the previous September, concentrated on the new technique that big red-faced sergeant-major was now going to demonstrate.

'Now then,' Ox-Jo continued, as the men who would fire the new device began to prepare their charges, 'you can see that slope up there is a medium-to-difficult ascent.' He indicated the sheer rock face that towered above them, two hundred metres high, with a forefinger like a small salami. 'Me, it would take perhaps half an hour to climb using conventional techniques. For you,' he added with a sneer, 'it'd be an hour at least. Too much of the old four against one in yer bunks at night, I shouldn't be surprised!' He made an obscene and explicit gesture with his right hand.

Corporal Jap Madad, Ox-Jo's running-mate, the wizened, slant-eyed issue of a fleeting relationship between the daughter of a Bavarian technician on the German-American reconnaissance of Nanga Parbat in 1920 and an amorous Hunza guide-porter, again simpered in his shrill falsetto, 'But I can't help it if I'm in love with my right fist, Sarnt-Major.'

Ox-Jo glared at him. 'Listen you Bavarian barn-shitter, you garden dwarf-with plush ears, you'll get a set of my knuckles in yer ugly yeller kisser if yer don't hold yer water!' But there was no rancour in Ox-Jo's voice. As always Jap, his pal, was trying to lower the tension; for what was going to come could be highly dangerous. He knew it and Jap did too.

The big sergeant-major turned to the trooper crouched over the discharger. 'All right?' he enquired.

'All right, Sarnt-Major,' the man answered.

'Right then, fire the thing!'

The trooper turned the wheel at the side of the discharger, bending his head hastily.

*A crack!* A spurt of flame. A small puff of bright white smoke. Suddenly the four-hooked steel grapnel that had been inside the tube burst out. It shot right up the steep slope at an alarming speed, ever upwards, snaking behind it length after length of stout alpine rope. The men gasped and Stuermer noted, his stopwatch in his hand now ready to start the timing, that they were suitably impressed. The device was obviously something new to them.

*Slap!* The hook hit the rock with a metallic echo. The rope quivered taut and fell still.

The confident grin disappeared from Ox-Jo's face and Stuermer knew instinctively what he was thinking. Had the grapnel embedded itself firmly enough in the rock? If it hadn't, then . . . but Stuermer didn't want to think that particular thought through to its decidedly unpleasant end.

Ox-Jo stalked to the end of the rope and, exerting all his strength, pulled hard. The grapnel held. He gave a satisfied snort. Turning to the troopers, he grunted, 'All right arses-with-ears, I want a volunteer to show you just how much weight that piece of tin up there can bear.' Before anyone could step forward the customary regulation one pace, Ox-Jo pointed his forefinger at Jap. 'You, you're allus opening yer big mouth and causing a draught, you're volunteering.'

Jap rolled his dark eyes in mock fear. 'Me, Sarnt-Major,' he protested, poking a dirty finger at his skinny chest, 'yer don't want me, do yer? You know I get dizzy at heights. Besides it's that time of the month for me.'

Ox-Jo crooked his finger at the little man. 'Another word from you, comrade, and you'll be lacking a set of ears. *Komm!*'

Like the condemned man being led to the gallows, Jap came.

Ox Jo bent down, inserted his huge arm between Jap's legs and swung the corporal effortlessly over his broad shoulder. With his right hand, he grasped the rope. 'Right, sir,' he called back to a waiting Stuermer with his stopwatch, 'ready when you are.'

Stuermer hesitated. If the grapnel didn't hold, or Ox-Jo made any kind of mistake, he would lose two of his most experienced climbers. Yet he knew *Stormtroop Edelweiss* had to continue to use these new techniques if they were going to keep ahead of any potential enemy. The utilization of the grapnel with all its inherent dangers could well mean that his men might beat the enemy in the race to capture some vital pass or peak. Stuermer tensed, gaze fixed on the stopwatch. As the little second hand raced round to sixty, he opened his mouth ready to give the command that would send Ox-Jo scuttling up the line towards the peak some two hundred metres above them. But that wasn't to be.

In exactly the same instant that the second hand hit the minute, Major Greul raced round the mountain bend, wildly scattering gravel and hard-frozen snow behind the rear wheel of his motorbike, roaring at the top of his voice, '*Stop, sir . . . stop . . .* We haven't a minute to lose! We're expected at the Führer's headquarters in exactly two hours – in full dress uniform!'

Happily, Jap tapped a perplexed Ox-Jo on the shoulder and said, 'Thank God for the Führer, now will you get your big dirty paws off'n my eggs? If you squeeze them any more, you'll have me turning into a shitting singing tenor . . .'

'Quick, fill me in!' Colonel Stuermer snapped, hastily buckling on his sword, as Ox-Jo drove the Volkswagen jeep in front of the officers' quarters and Greul pulled on his dress gloves, admiring himself in the mirror.

He didn't like his second-in-command. Gottfried Greul did not climb mountains, as he, the professional, did because 'they were there!' He climbed to conquer, as a patriotic duty, to show to the decadent Western World the strength, the power, the invincibility of the new young National Socialist Germany. From that day in 1931 when he had conquered the North Face of the Eiger as a short-trousered Hitler Youth leader and shocked the Swiss by planting the hated crooked-cross flag on its snowy summit, Greul had regarded climbing as a political act: the conquest of each new mountain a symbol of the unbeatable strength of the new creed.

All the same, Stuermer told himself as he completed buckling on the absurd dress sword for the reception by the Führer just across the old pre-war 1938 frontier with Austria, 'the East Mark', as it was now called, Major Greul was one of the world's finest climbers and a brave soldier, too. He could have had a worse officer as his second-in-command, even though Greul was a fanatical Nazi.

Satisfied with the way he had pulled on his grey chamois gloves, Greul turned from the mirror. 'Unfortunately, sir,' he said, 'the balloon has gone up again – without *Stormtroop Edelweiss*.'

Stuermer shot him a sharp look. 'What is that supposed to mean, Major?' he barked.

'Norway, sir! According to the signal I received an hour ago from Corps HQ of the Alpine Corps, our Führer in all his wisdom has decided to save Norway from being invaded by perfidious Albion.'

'Save Norway? What in three devils' name are you talking about, man?'

'This, sir,' Greul replied unperturbed, reaching for his dress cap, while outside Ox-Jo honked the horn urgently. 'That old Tommy umbrella man and his toady the drunken decadent sot Churchill, First Lord of the Admiralty, had planned to invade Norway so that they could cut off the iron ore coming to the Reich via Narvik. The Führer, in his infinite wisdom, knew of this.'

Greul sucked in his breath, full of respect at the holy name and Stuermer barked, 'God in Heaven, man, get on with it – what the hell has happened?'

'As I was saying,' Greul went on, 'the Führer decided that our glorious *Wehrmacht*, cost what it may, had to be sent to Norway to protect our Nordic cousins from the English pirates. That was done yesterday and,' he frowned suddenly and stopped, his high brow furrowed, as if with frustration.

'Well, go on. Piss or get off the pot!' Stuermer said, using the crude soldiers' expression.

'Part of the Alpine Corps under General Dietl landed at Narvik twenty-four hours ago and . . . and something has gone wrong,' Greul blurted out.

'*Wrong?*' Stuermer echoed, feeling a sense of shock. Hitler had done it again. He instinctively knew that he and his men would soon be involved in yet another crazy mission for him, the Greatest Captain of All Times, as the *Edelweiss* troopers called their 'Führer' contemptuously.

'Yes, sir. I don't know exactly what. All I know, sir, is that we've got the red alert.' He stared proudly at his CO 'And *Stormtroop Edelweiss* will be going into action again . . .'

# TWO

It had taken them an hour to cross from Kufstein in Bavaria into Austria, motoring swiftly with hardly any traffic on the winding mountain road through the Ostertal before beginning the long slow climb up to the 'Eagle's Nest,' Hitler's mountain-top home. Thereafter it had taken them nearly half an hour to pass through check-point after check-point, guarded by gigantic black-clad SS guards, hard-faced and unsmiling the lot of them.

'Shitting parade-ground soldiers,' Ox-Jo at the wheel had grumbled. 'I'd like to get them in the shitting mountains. I'd soon show them what real soldiering is!'

Now Greul and Stuermer waited in one of the ante-rooms, watched by watchful SS adjutants, who were so tall that they dwarfed even the two mountaineers.

Officers with important-looking folders marked, '*Geheime Reichssache*'[1] sped back and forth. Behind the doors of the offices, telephones rang incessantly. Generals and admirals, faces set and grim, popped in and out, as if they were in a great hurry. Once even Bormann, Hitler's secretary, bullet-headed and fat, looking like a rundown boxer, poked his shaven skull round a door to see who was in the ante-room. He saw the mountain officers and nodded, as if the fact that they were there was of some importance.

'Flap,' Stuermer whispered out of the side of his mouth, not taking his gaze off one of the blond, gigantic SS adjutants who was watching them, as if he expected them to steal one of the solid silver ashtrays which were spread about the place.

[1] Top secret.

Greul frowned. 'I suppose so, sir.' He bit his bottom lip, as if he could not comprehend how his beloved Führer could possibly have made a mistake.

Stuermer grinned suddenly. It did him good to see his second-in-command's faith in the Führer shaken.

Suddenly the tall twin doors to the right were flung open. An SS captain, who was a head taller than the rest of the adjutants, called, blue eyes fixed on some distant horizon, '*Meine Herren, der Führer lasst bitten!*' He stood to one side and extended a hand, as if to usher them inside, bowing slightly like some stage butler in a third-rate comedy.

Greul and Stuermer pressed their dress caps more tightly under their arms, grasped their swords and, in step, marched smartly across the ante-room into Hitler's huge study, dominated by the celebrated picture window, always shown in the newsreels, which offered a spectacular view of the mountains stretching from Austria right into Bavaria, thirty kilometres away.

Adolf Hitler posed over the huge map table, nickel-framed spectacles tilted at the end of his nose, framed by the usual coterie. Bormann, Keitel, his military adviser, Admiral Raeder, the head of the fleet, old-fashioned and pompous in his wing collar, and Jodl, the Führer's chief-of-staff, his normally pale, cunning face unusually flushed this day. Hitler looked up at the two newcomers, eyes blank. Then he saw the insignia of the Mountain Corps and a look almost of hope swept across his pale face. '*Stormtroop Edelweiss*?' he inquired urgently, revealing his yellow teeth.

Stuermer clicked his heels together as regulations required, and barked in that Prussian parade ground tone which he hated, '*Oberstleutnant Stuermer, Sturmabteiling Edelweiss-zur Stelle, mein Führer!*'

Hitler hardly gave him time to finish the ritual. He slipped off his glasses, hurried around the table, and to Stuermer's surprise, clasped the big colonel's right hand in both his flabby, damp hands. 'It is good – exceedingly good – of you to come, Colonel Stuermer,' he said exuberantly, in his excitement his Austrian accent thicker than ever.

Stuermer muttered something and the next instant found himself being led through the assembled officers by Hitler himself, while Greul, his eyes blazing with pride, followed.

Hitler paused dramatically at the map of Northern Europe spread out on the table and rapped it with the knuckles of his right hand, still holding on to Stuermer with his other one. 'Norway,' he rasped, 'vitally important for our iron ore supplies from Sweden and as a strategic position for our final blow against the decadent British to bring their vaunted Empire to its knees. Thirty-six hours ago, we invaded the country to protect it from an assault by the English. Our landings at Oslo, Trondheim, Bergen, Narvik were all completely successful. Indeed, your own General Dietl with two thousand of your comrades landed at Narvik to an official welcome by the local Norwegian commander.' He looked up at Stuermer as if he expected to see some reaction to his words, but there was none on the mountaineer's handsome face, only cold military reserve.

But behind that façade, Stuermer's brain raced. So Hitler had done it again, just as he had with Austria, Czechoslovakia and Poland. But this time something had gone wrong and he didn't need a crystal ball to tell him that the skinny-framed commander of the Alpine Division had gone and landed himself, as Ox-Jo would have phrased it, 'right up to his hooter in shit!'

Hitler's next words confirmed his forebodings. 'Unfortunately, bad weather, snow and ice and the like, has prevented the main body of our troops from coming up the peninsula from Oslo and, as yet, linking up with General Dietl. At this very moment my brave Dietl and two thousand of his men are cut off in Narvik, with no artillery to speak of – our intelligence was wrong when it predicted that the Norwegians would have coastal batter-

## NORWEGIAN THEATRE OF OPERATIONS
## April-June 1940

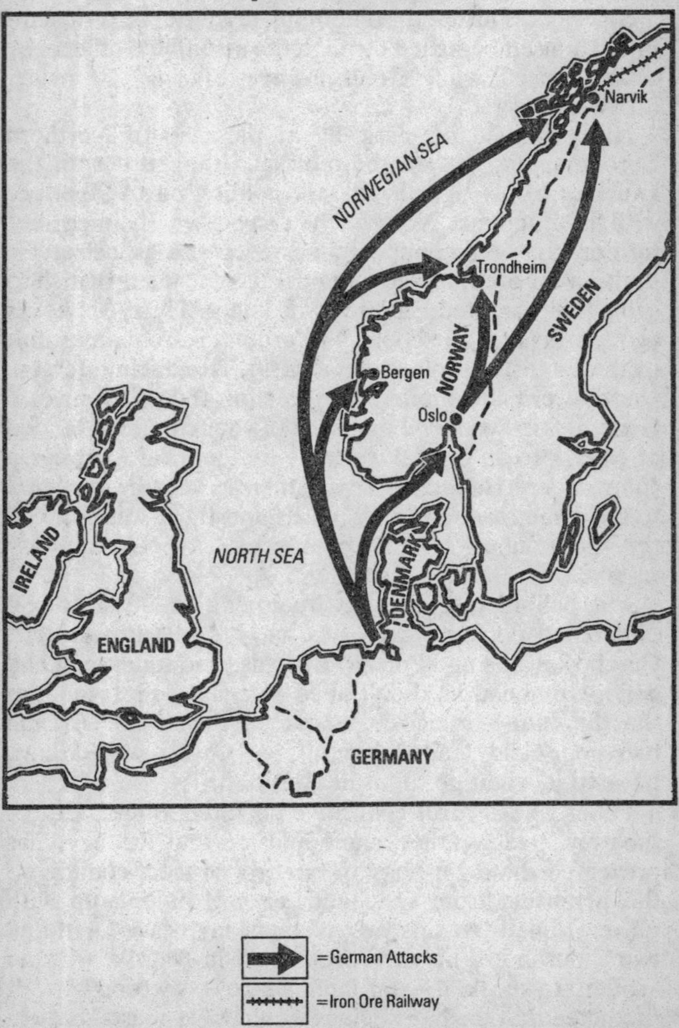

ies there which we could use – save for the guns of the ten destroyers of the *Kriegsmarine*[1] which brought his force.'

Hitler paused for breath and Stuermer said, 'I see, *mein Führer*,' though he didn't one bit. What had Dietl's plight got to do with him and *Stormtroop Edelweiss*?

'Now this,' Hitler barked, his eyes blazing abruptly. He clicked his fingers.

Keitel, fat, pompous, ramrod-straight, like the lackey he was, picked up a battered briefcase to which was attached what appeared to be a shrunken human hand linked to it by a bloodstained chain. Hurriedly, he pulled out the sheath of papers it contained, the top one marked, in red, '*MOST SECRET*.'

Hitler accepted it from the field marshal without a word of thanks. Keitel behaved like a lackey and was obviously treated like one by Hitler. The Führer tapped the papers, 'Secret instructions prepared in London, and picked up from a dead British courier officer yesterday afternoon. General Dietl saw their importance at once and had them flown to me immediately.'

Again, feeling ever more stupid, Stuermer repeated that idiotic, 'I see, *mein Führer*.'

'They were bound for the headquarters of King Haakon, who has fled his capital and is reported to be somewhere south of Narvik.[2] They contain detailed instructions for the Norwegians about co-operation between them and the English.'

'You mean the English are going to land troops in Norway too, *mein Führer*?' Greul gasped, too excited at the news, which promised action at last, to be awed by the presence of the great man.

Hitler nodded gloomily. 'Exactly.' Behind him the man who had planned the attack looked down at his gleaming riding boots as if ashamed; Major-General Jodl, Hitler's

[1] German Navy.
[2] King of Norway in 1940.

planning genius, was obviously out of favour at the moment.

'According to the translation of the documents,' the Führer continued, 'the English plan to land expeditionary forces here at the port of Mamsos, some two hundred kilometres north-east of Trondheim,' he tapped the map angrily, 'and here at Andalsnes one hundred and fifty kilometres to the south-west. Obviously, their aim is to capture Trondheim and cut it off from our forces moving up from the south. I have already taken certain steps to ensure that they do not realize that aim. Five thousand men are on their way to Trondheim as reinforcements.'

Greul breathed a sigh of admiration at Hitler's genius, but Stuermer waited tensely, his apprehension growing by the second. Hitler had not ordered them to the Eagle's Nest to demonstrate just how brilliant he was. There was something else to come, he knew it.

Hitler's voice sank. 'The other part of the Englishmen's plan is far more serious,' he continued. 'From the documents, it is clear that they intend to attack us from the sea. A large force of their ships, including carriers and at least one capital ship, is already on its way, destination,' he hesitated for a fraction of a second, as if it hurt to utter the word, '*Narvik!* What is their aim?' Hitler answered his own question. 'To destroy the naval force of our own destroyers – ten in number – which took Dietl's men to Narvik, isolate him completely up there and prepare for landings to take him and Narvik.' He let his words sink in and Stuermer could see from the looks on the faces of the high-ranking officers standing around the map table that they all shared Hitler's fears; obviously they had been discussing the matter all the while they had been waiting outside in the ante-room. 'We cannot allow this to happen, gentlemen,' Hitler continued. 'I would rather order General Dietl to retreat across the border into Sweden and allow himself and his men to be interned there by the Swedes than have them captured by the English.'

There was a subdued murmur of protest from the officers behind him, but Hitler appeared not to notice. Instead, he said, 'However, I am confident, gentlemen, that it won't come to that. I have already ordered General Student to prepare a battalion of his parachutists for a drop to the rear of Narvik so that they can reinforce Dietl, *and*,' he looked straight at Stuermur, using that old trick of his with which the tall mountaineer was going to become familiar in years to come, attempting to dominate him with those dark magnetic eyes of his, 'I am also going to employ your men, *mein lieber Oberst*.'

Angrily Stuermer shook his head, as if physically attempting to shake off that hypnotic gaze, 'How, *mein Führer*?' he snapped, while Greul waited for his beloved Leader's answer in tense expectation.

'Like this . . .'

But before Adolf Hitler could explain any further, the great door was flung open unceremoniously and the giant blond adjutant who had escorted the two mountaineer officers in stood there, his face blanched, eyes wild and wide with shock. '*Mein Führer*,' he stammered, failing even to click to attention and give the 'German greeting'[1], '*mein Führer*, I am sorry, but it is vital you should know . . .'

'Know what?' Hitler snapped angrily.

'It's the English, sir, they've . . .'

'Out with it, man!' Hitler snorted.

'Sir, it's a signal from naval command, Narvik,' the words came out in an excited flow, 'the English have been sighted off the coast. *They're coming in for the attack!*'

[1] i.e. the Hitler salute.

# THREE

The five grey shapes moved steadily through the dark-green water of the fiord, the high, snow-covered mountains glimpsed in the occasional gaps in the cruel sleet which lashed the faces of the lookouts and the men tensed on the open bridges. The destroyers' tripods and rigging were already white with glistening hoar frost, while the swaying decks were ankle-deep in freezing slush. But the men huddled in the gun-turrets, muffled in their asbestos anti-flash gear, or crouched over the torpedo tubes, were wide awake, their every nerve tingling electrically. For all of them knew this dawn that they were sailing right into the German-held port and that they were outnumbered two to one. The only way they were going to pull it off this April morning was by surprising the Germans, hitting them hard and fast before they had woken up to what was happening to them.

On the bridge of the *Hardy*, flotilla-commander Captain Warburton-Lee, square-faced and with his dark hair parted in the middle in the fashion of the twenties, nodded to the waiting signaller. 'All right, Sparks, send this to their Lordships. *Attacking at dawn . . . high water.*'

At his side on the swaying unprotected bridge, Paymaster-Lieutenant Stanning, his secretary, muffled up to the eyes in a brown fleecy dufflecoat, grinned. It was typical of the 'Old Man' – he never wasted a word even when he was communicating with no less a person than Winston Churchill, the First Lord of the Admiralty. Five words to explain a complicated tactical manoeuvre – going into the attack at dawn in order to achieve surprise, and at high water as protection from mines suspended by cables at the bottom of the narrow fiord.

Sparks sped away to relay the message to London, and

now all of them on the bridge concentrated again on spotting the first enemy vessel, as the five destroyers passing through the still dawn like grey ghosts came ever closer to the port of Narvik.

Five minutes later the tension was broken at last. Abruptly the storm of flying sleet cleared for an instant. Less than five hundred yards away, the unmistakably sleek shape of a *Moewe* class destroyer lying at anchor, leapt into view.

Warburton-Lee reacted immediately. 'There she is, Stanning!' he yelled like an excited schoolboy. '*A Boche destroyer!*' He swung round to the helmsman gripping the wheel with knuckles that were tensed white. 'Hard a-port!' he barked. 'Torpedo-room, stand by to fire.' Stanning could see he was having difficulty containing himself until the torpedo room had made the correct adjustments, then he snapped, '*Fire!*'

One . . . two . . . three, the tin fish, each containing a ton of high explosive, slid into the dark-green water. Stanning flung a quick look over the bridge. He caught a fleeting stream of bubbles and heard the hiss of compressed air; then they were gone, heading straight for the unsuspecting German destroyer.

At his side, Warburton-Lee started to count off the seconds. '*One . . . two . . . three . . .*'

All of a sudden there was a thick, throaty, muffled crump. The enemy destroyer leapt out of the water, or so it seemed, like a live thing. Seconds later it heeled over violently, its superstructure almost touching the water, thick white smoke streaming from its ruptured boilers. At once the air was filled with shouts, orders, piteous cries for help, as the German vessel started to sink, stern first.

'We've hit the bugger!' Warburton-Lee cried exuberantly.

'Yessir,' Stanning echoed, just as excited as the skipper, 'and first shot, too!'

Now the rest of the little flotilla hurtled forward seeking

the enemy anchored just beyond, darting to port and starboard in their search for targets of opportunity. The *Hunter* raced through the *Hardy*'s wake, her sharp, knifelike prow hitting each wave and shuddering violently as if it were a brick wall. A fat-bellied German merchantman, heavy in the water with iron ore from Swedish mines, loomed up out of the mist. The *Hunter*'s torpedo-room couldn't miss. Its first torpedo struck home. With the great hollow boom of metal striking metal, the merchantman broke apart instantly. She started to sink to the hoarse cheers of the men hanging on for their lives on *Hardy*'s swaying deck.

'Look out below!' the signaller yelled from the crow's nest. 'Torpedo on port bow!'

'*Hard over!*' Warburton-Lee screamed frantically.

The *Hardy* swung to the side, reeling madly. Its screws churned the water into a frantic white lather. Warburton-Lee grabbed a stanchion to prevent himself from falling, as the German torpedo streaked by with only yards to spare. A minute later, it crashed onto the shore beyond. One ton of high explosive went up with a tremendous roar, throwing sand and shingle straight upwards in a whirling wild column one hundred feet high.

Now *Hardy* and the other four destroyers were running wild, deep in the fiord. All was controlled confusion on the British ships as gunners strapped behind their 'Chicago pianos', high, banked batteries of massed machine guns, peppered the shore, the 4.5 inch guns thundered and the torpedo men set their tin fish whirring on their lethal course to left and right. Decks trembled as the little grey ships raced all out, given the benefit of their 30,000hp. The whole vessel vibrated like a wild thing. Scarlet flame stabbed the grey gloom. On all sides there was the swift orange burst of exploding shells and the sudden dramatic start of yet another fire.

But now the surprised Germans were beginning to react. On shore the quick-firing 20mm cannon, banked in batteries of four, started to pump their shells at the

British at a rate of 1,000 a minute. Tracer, white, red and green, raced across the narrow stretch of water in a highly lethal morse. On the burning German destroyers, brave gunners fought to the last, still firing as the icy-cold water crept higher in the turrets, until finally they were submerged.

Captain Warburton-Lee, right in the middle of it, the deck of his ship littered with empty yellow shellcases, his eyes burning with the acrid fumes of gunsmoke, knew it was time to go – he had done what he had come here to do. Grimly he held on as two wildly whirling spouts of water bracketed his ship and rocked it from side to side, as if it had been punched by some gigantic fist. 'The Jerries are ranging in, Stanning!' he yelled above the tremendous racket and the wild thump-thump of the massed machine guns. 'Think we'd better make tracks while the going's good!'

Stanning nodded his head. He was unable to speak. Dabbing his bloodshot eyes, he asked himself why in heaven's name had he abandoned the safety of the paymaster's cabin and volunteered to help out here on the bridge. He needed his head seeing to!

Now the brave flags started to race up *Hardy*'s mast, as she signalled her companions to withdraw. They swept round in tight wild curves, their sterns almost disappearing in the great whirling rush of water their screws churned up. Almost in unison, their captains ordered, 'Full speed' and, at thirty knots an hour, leaving behind them death and destruction, and the whole waterfront burning angrily, they sped towards the open sea.

Warburton-Lee whistled happily through his teeth, not noticing the burning wind on his broad face. They had done it! They had destroyed the Boche without losing a single ship or a single man; and already the snow was returning. It would cover them against any Jerry air attack; for the Jerries dominated the air over Norway, that was for sure.

'Well, Stanning,' he began in a high good mood to his

paymaster, 'I think the matelots deserve a little bit of Nelson's blood'.[1] He stopped short, eyes filled with sudden alarm.

Three lean grey shapes had appeared to port. And there was no mistaking that stark black and red flag with its crooked-cross symbol.

'*Jerries!*' Stanning yelled.

The alarm bells shrilled again. The sweating, exhausted gunners flung themselves behind their weapons once more, knee-deep in gleaming yellow shellcases. But this time the Germans were quicker. Their 12.7cm erupted and ugly yellow and red flame ran the length of their heaving decks. At that range they simply couldn't miss. With a frenzied, unnerving screech, enemy shells roared flatly across the fiord. Stanning tensed for what must come.

The *Hardy* reeled violently as she was hit by the first salvo. The bridge seemed to disintegrate and suddenly there were wounded and dying men everywhere. Stanning pulled himself to his feet. Next to him lay three seamen, all dead, arms flung out in abandoned postures. He stared at them in a daze, unable to take in the fact that their young lives had been snuffed out so abruptly. Suddenly his nostrils picked up the smell of burning and the acrid fumes escaping from ruptured electric batteries. 'Christ,' he cried aloud, the noise and screams suddenly assailing him with full force, '*we've been hit!*'

He flung a wild glance around the shattered bridge, with smoking debris lying in confused chaotic heaps everywhere. Still groggy with shock, he staggered over to where the navigation officer Gordon Smith lay on his back, blood trickling out of the side of his mouth, down his suddenly pinched and ashen cheek. 'Are you all right, Gordon?' he gasped.

The navigation officer's eyes flickered open momentarily. He opened his lips to say something and still more dark red blood spilled out between his gleaming white

[1] Rum.

teeth. Suddenly his eyeballs rolled a bright white. His head slipped to one side gently. He was dead.

Stanning rose to his feet slowly, unable to take it in. Almost thoughtfully, he wiped the scum from his lips and turned to the skipper.

Captain Warburton-Lee was dying. His uniform was tattered and charred everywhere. His shirt was already pink with blood and his face was gory with it. Blood spurted constantly from a gaping wound in his side, marking every heartbeat with a thick scarlet jet. Stanning was galvanized into action. He bent down. Raising the captain's head, he cried desperately, 'Captain . . . Captain Warburton-Lee . . .'

The skipper looked up at him, eyes wet with pain, but calm. 'I've had it, Stanning,' he whispered. 'If the ship's finished, give orders . . . to abandon.' Warburton-Lee's voice was fading fast, 'Give the chaps a chance . . .'

The paymaster-lieutenant who, when he had volunteered for a spell on the bridge, had never dreamed he would soon be commanding the *Hardy*, as her sole surviving officer, flung a wild glance around him. Their sister ship the *Havock* was trying desperately to lay a protective smoke screen around the crippled, already sinking *Hardy*, which was losing speed by the instant. A thousand yards away the *Hunter*, also badly hit by the surprise attack from the three Germans, was burning fiercely. He could not expect any help from them. He would have to manage the best he could by himself. Ducking as yet another great shell tore the air apart and exploded a hundred yards away, showering the crippled ship with water, he doubled down to the wheelhouse.

The rating in charge hung dead over the wheel, blood dripping like persistent rain to the pool at his feet. Savagely, Stanning pushed him to one side. The veins standing out at his temples, sweat gleaming in fat pearls at his eyebrows, Stanning exerted all his strength. The wheel answered. The *Hardy* stopped going round in circles. In a paroxysm of frenzied fear, he headed the ship for the shore; for he knew instinctively she would never make the open sea now. He had to beach her!

The ship reeled alarmingly. From below came the reverberating boom of metal on metal and the faint screams of agony as the scalding hot steam started to escape from her ruptured boilers. Stanning bit his lip and tried to forget the terrible fate of the stokers trapped in the engine room.

'Abandon ship,' he yelled at the top of his voice, '*abandon ship . . . do you hear . . . ABANDON SHIP . . .*'

Slowly the stricken *Hardy* started to move to the shore, some three hundred yards away, taking in water all the time, as her speed lessened dramatically.

Stanning gripped the wheel until it hurt, willing her to make it, forcing her ever closer. She *had* to make it. 'Better get the captain over the side,' he flung over his shoulder, eyes fixed on that beach as if it were the Promised Land itself. 'He's still alive.'

The dying skipper was hurriedly lowered onto the little raft, as the *Hardy* came ever closer to the beach, with the Germans sensing victory, slamming shell after shell into the ship.

A crunch, a crash. Stanning held on grimly. There was the terrifying ear-piercing shriek of escaping steam. Flames spurted high in the air. For one terrifying instant, the frightful carnage and damage was illuminated with the startling clarity of a photographer's magnesium flash. Stanning, bleeding from multiple wounds, sank to the deck. He had made it.

'*Hurrah . . . hurrah . . .*' the excited *Gebirgsjager*[1] cried, as the enemy destroyer reeled to a stop on the beach across the fiord, greedy flames running the length of her shattered frame. 'That showed the Tommies. *Hurrah!*'

[1] Alpine troops.

Skinny, tall General Dietl, their commander, peak cap set at a jaunty angle on his close-cropped head, slowly lowered his binoculars. He didn't share his excited men's happiness at the victory. For a moment that last picture of the crazed English sailors running along the deck, pursued by that searing blow-torch of flame, their uniforms already ablaze, lived on in his mind's eye. Then, professional soldier that he was, he forgot the horror and concentrated on his own position. Five of the destroyers which had brought him to Narvik were sunk or sinking, plus three of the merchantmen. His total artillery force, therefore, had been reduced by fifty per cent. If the Tommies came back, and he was sure they would, and began landing troops, now that he had only thirty naval cannon to defend himself from a seaborne landing, he was sunk. He needed help – and he damn well needed it *immediately!*

Suddenly alarmed beyond all measure, his normal professional coolness vanished completely, he cried, a note of hysteria in his deep Bavarian voice, 'Signaller . . . a message to the OKW[1] . . . immediately . . . at *the double now* . . .'

[1] German High Command.

# FOUR

Ox-Jo spoke for them all. He looked at the big, broken-nosed para and said, 'Do you mean to stand there like a wet fart waiting to hit the thunderbox wall and tell me that you lot put that big umbrella on yer backs and step out – *into mid-air, one thousand metres up!*' Ox-Jo's eyes bulged from his crimson face in absolute, total, disbelief.

The para NCO who was demonstrating the chute nodded happily. ''Cos, we do get paid a bit extra for it,' he conceded in his thick Berlin accent.

Ox-Jo looked around the faces of the troopers and said, 'There ain't enough money in the whole of the *Reichsbank* to make Mrs Meier's handsome son use one of them things. Hell, I'd be ripe for the rubber wagon, if I did that.'

'You *could* drop without one, Sarnt-Major,' the Berliner suggested helpfully. 'They tell me you Bavarians have got hard arses – and even harder heads. Perhaps you don't need chutes after all?'

Ox-Jo doubled his redoubtable fist threateningly. 'Watch yer lip, *comrade*,' he snarled, 'or you might be needing a new set of choppers!'

Colonel Stuermer stepped in hastily, as behind him on the tower another trainee paratrooper flung himself into nothing, to drop a terrifying one hundred metres until the tethered parachute grabbed him and stopped his wild descent. 'Button it up, you great horned ox!' he snapped hurriedly. 'You all know the urgency of our mission and the fact that we can't waste time – or risk casualties – in practice drops. We drop the first time and the only time. That's the drill which has been decided for us at the Führer's HQ and that's the way it's going to be.' He nodded to the broken-nosed para sergeant, his ugly face wreathed in an unholy grin at the sight of the mountaineers' ashen faces. 'Carry on with the instruction, Sergeant.'

'Thank you, sir. All right, *gentlemen*,' he emphasized the word with an undisguised sneer in Ox-Jo's direction, 'this is how the chute works. This is the static line, that's what we call it. It's hooked to the anchor cable in the Junkers itself. Then there's a length of rope three to four metres long attached to the parachute canopy. As the parachutist jumps from the Junkers, he's thrown outwards to the port wing. The prop wash then forces him to the end of the static line. The resulting tug pulls the cover from the pack tray, exposing the canopy. At that moment the rope, the one I just told you about, begins to pull out the chute . . .' The para NCO went on and on happily, obviously savouring the looks of growing alarm on his listeners' faces as they started to comprehend what was going to happen to them *soon*, an unspoken question slowly dawning on all of them.

'Hey,' Ox-Jo interrupted firmly, '*nun ein bisschen langsam . . .*' He gulped and then voiced that unspoken question, 'What happens if all this paraphernalia *don't* shitting well work?' He looked menacingly at the para sergeant, 'Tell me that, mate. What do we do then?'

The sergeant was in no way put out. 'What do you do then, mate?' he echoed, forehead creased in a frown, as if he were seriously considering Ox-Jo's query. 'Well, I'll tell yer. Yer close yer glassy orbs, lay yer pinkies on yer manly chest and,' his voice rose for the punchline, '*make a beautiful corpse!*' He doubled up, tears streaming down his crimson face, entranced by his own humour.

Stuermer shook his head in disbelief and then, turning, walked away, telling himself that it was probably an opportune time to leave them to it. Ox-Jo's face was turning a livid beetroot colour. In a minute he would explode.

*

At the base of the control tower at Hamburg-Fuhlsbuttel Field, which they had turned into an emergency headquarters for the new op, telephones jingled incessantly and pale-faced clerks in *Luftwaffe* uniform hurried back and forth or banged away at typewriters, as if their very lives depended upon it. Down the side of one wall, their *Luftwaffe* hosts had erected a huge map of the Norwegian battlefront and, Stuermer noted in passing, it was already covered with a rash of blue and red crayon marks which indicated, he knew, their own and the enemy positions. He nodded glumly to himself. Hitler's new adventure was obviously not going as smoothly as he had originally planned. There was already a lot of fighting going on, especially to the south above Oslo, and there was going to be a lot more before this spring was out.

He opened the door to his own little office, where Greul and Major Stiebel, a cocky, bowlegged pilot who was in charge of the Junkers transports, stood bent over the large relief map of northern Norway that they had dug up in a Hamburg junk shop near the waterfront that very morning. The two officers clicked to attention politely but, with an impatient wave of his hand, Stuermer ordered them to stand at ease. There was no time for all that Prussian military nonsense now. The lives of his men were at stake and he had little time for playing games.

'Well, gentlemen, what is the situation?' he snapped, slinging his peak-cap onto the battered leather armchair in the far corner of the little office.

Greul spoke first. 'General Dietl reported thirty minutes ago that another British naval force has been sighted off the Westfjord, obviously poised for a further attack on his remaining ships.'

Stuermer flashed a look at the bowlegged major who looked like an old-style cavalryman in his baggy riding breeches and gleaming boots. For some reason the air force major even wore a sword. He answered Stuermer's unspoken question in harsh clipped bursts, as if his words were bullets and he a machine gun. 'Air impossible, *Herr Oberst* . . . Fog, rain and sleet. Visibility . . . virtually nil . . . Our planes can't attack them . . . General Dietl and his ships are . . . on their own.' His rat-trap mouth, worked as if by steel springs, slapped close.

Stuermer frowned. The man talked like some caricature of an old Imperial Army Prussian subaltern; but Greul was obviously impressed. In *his* opinion Major Stiebel talked like a real soldier. 'It's also reported from Narvik that the Navy's B-Service[1] have picked up radio signals that indicate another large force of enemy ships are in the same general area, probably troop transports, according to the people in Kiel. So we can conclude . . .'

'. . . That the Tommies are going to land troops after the second naval attack and that we will have to go ahead with this damnfool adventure.' Stuermer beat him to it, angry with the whole damned world at this particular moment.

'Yessir,' Greul answered a little crestfallen, as if he was puzzled at his CO's anger. Why should Stuermer be angry when they had this glorious opportunity for action once again?

Stuermer did not seem to notice. Instead he studied the relief map, trying to put himself in the place of their unknown English enemy. What would they do? After all, they were operating nearly a thousand kilometres from their nearest base in the Shetlands, without Dietl's local air cover, though they could bring up an aircraft carrier, he supposed, and chance attacks by the land-based German Stukas.

It was obvious what their main objective would be – the single-tracked railway line from Sweden which brought Germany her all-important iron ore. Even if Hitler did capture the rest of the Norwegian peninsula, if the Tommies could grab that line and Narvik, too, for they would need a port to maintain their hold on it, they would have achieved an important victory.

[1] Radio-interception service.

Stuermer sucked his teeth and thought on. Naturally, Dietl would abandon the port if the railway line were threatened. With his two thousand mountaineers and whatever sailors he could arm from the sunken destroyers, he would not be able to hold both. Thereupon the British would land troops in the port too. So the overwhelming question was – where would the Tommies land first? And that raised another question: where could *Stormtroop Edelweiss* do the most good in this whole damned nasty mess that Hitler had got the *Gebirgsjager* into?

He stared hard at the relief map, while the two majors waited almost apprehensively. Outside an affected voice was saying, 'My God, Otto, some of these stubble-hoppers are really the limit! The fellow only wanted a second helping of peasoup, complete with an extra sausage. I ask you, Otto, *an extra sausage!* What next?'

Naturally the English would use conventional tactics. Soldiers, he had come to realize ever since he had been torn away from his beloved mountains to form and lead *Edelweiss*, always did. They would come in on both sides of the port in a pincer movement. Dietl would react by withdrawing along the railway line. The English would react, in their turn, by extending their pincer movement by attempting to come in behind the railway line, pushing forward through the narrow gap between it and the high plateau beyond. He clicked his fingers suddenly and Major Stiebel started visibly.

'Major Stiebel,' Stuermer snapped, knowing instinctively he had found the right solution, 'could your men land my group here,' he stabbed the central plateau to the east of the railway line with his forefinger, 'or roughly in that general area, but not too far from the railway?'

Stiebel looked at him aghast. For a moment his Prussian officer manner deserted the bowlegged air force officer. 'But a para-landing in that area would entail a thousand dangers and imponderables. Thermals, the fact that the terrain could well split your outfit into scattered little groups, cut off from each other, the difficulty of gaining sufficient height for my old Auntie Jus, the . . .'[1]

'*Can you?*' Stuermer broke in brutally, his face set and stern.

Stiebel swallowed hard and then pulled himself together. Clicking to attention, he barked, as if he were on a parade ground, eyes fixed woodenly on some distant horizon. 'Can do, sir!'

Stuermer wasted no more time. 'Major Greul . . . Major Stiebel . . . alert your commands. We fly tonight. There is no more time to be wasted.'

Outside the prissy-voiced *Luftwaffe* clerk was saying, 'Of course, what can you expect from common working-class people like them. They don't know any better, do they, Otto?'

[1] Nickname for the Junkers 52 transport planes used by the German paratroops during WW II.

# FIVE

'Narvik,' the pilot's voice crackled metallically, 'to port.' He laughed harshly and added quickly, 'For the benefit of you stubble-hoppers that means – *to your left!*'

Colonel Stuermer smiled and, bending his head, peered out of the Junkers' window.

Far down below there was the faint silver glint of water with, here and there, slow, heavy columns of black smoke. He screwed up his eyes and thought he could just make out a fat grey shape lying at the edge of the water. Probably one of Dietl's wrecked destroyers, he told himself, and then forgot Narvik as the cloud closed in again and they continued their slow progress to the high plateau.

Up front, the sergeant-despatcher in his baggy coveralls continued his little lecture to the men of Stuermer's HQ, all now dressed in similar overalls, appearing humpbacked in their parachutes.

'We call it rolling up the stick,' he was saying, 'a means of keeping a stick of paras together once they have jumped, 'cos otherwise they can easily get spread out over kilometres – and, comrades, I don't envy anybody who gets cut off on his lonesome down there. If the cold and hunger don't get him, the wolves will.'

'Get on with it,' Jap growled from his position on the bench next to Ox-Jo, 'you're making me piss myself!'

The despatcher tugged the end of his red swollen drinker's nose, and grinned. 'Don't say I didn't warn you then,' he quipped. 'Well, this is how you roll up the stick. The first members of the stick to jump note the direction of the "aircraft stream", as soon as they hit the dirt, and follow it. The soldiers who drop last move *against* the direction, while the middle members of the stick stand firm and wait till the two ends meet them. Clear?'

'Clear as mud!' Jap snorted.

Ox-Jo growled, 'Listen, sauce-hound, all I'm shitting well concerned about is getting Mrs Meier's handsome son down in one piece. Christ Almighty, what with this chute, thirty kilos of personal equipment, plus another shitting thirty in that kitbag I'm going to have tied to my right leg, when I hit the deck I'm sure I'll go right through and come out in shitting Australia!'

The despatcher grinned again, though Stuermer noticed his right hand tapping the back pocket of his baggy pants furtively, as if he were reassuring himself that his 'flatman', half-filled with cheap *kognak*, was still there. Obviously, he was nervous – and *he* wasn't even going to jump!

Stuermer frowned as the full impact of what they were soon going to do hit him once more. With merely two hours of theoretical instruction behind them, they were going to step out into mid-air and drop into one of the most inhospitable landscapes in the world. There in that harsh, brutal terrain, cold and forbidding under the best of climatic conditions, their only shelter their tents and possibly a few stunted birch trees, they were going to establish a defensive position to hold back any large-scale attempt made by the British to squeeze to the east of the vital railway line and turf Dietl out. It was a tall order, a very tall order indeed.

Stuermer sucked his teeth and stared around at the bronzed, tough faces of his troopers. If anyone could do it, they could, and it was the kind of assignment for which their whole upbringing and military training had prepared them: the individualist's battle, not only against man, their enemy, but against nature itself, in all its beautiful savagery. For a moment Hitler's last words flashed through his mind. As the Führer had pressed his hands warmly, just before he and Greul left his HQ, 'Stuermer,' he had declared, his husky Austrian voice vibrant with pent-up emotion, 'if anyone can do it, it will be you and your *Edelweiss*, for you are . . . *my eagles in the snow!*'

Five minutes later the red warning light up front began to wink off and on. Stuermer knew what it meant. They were approaching the dropping zone. He flashed a last look out of the little window. The rest of the formation was still there, flying in a great V through the scudding cloud, coming ever closer to the snow-capped, inhospitable peaks below.

The despatcher turned his back and took a quick swig of his flatman.

Ox-Jo nudged Jap. 'Cast yer glassy orbs on that, apeturd, will yer?' he growled enviously. 'That shit fills his guts with good old sauce – and we're doing the shitting jumping, with not even a quick wet to speed us on our way!'

'Tough shit,' Jap said unsympathetically, for he knew that his running-mate had filled both his water-bottles with tea and rum, though unfortunately for the big NCO, they were buried so deep beneath the rest of his equipment that he couldn't get at them. 'Write a letter of protest to the Führer.'

Angrily, Ox-Jo stuck up a middle finger the size of a small salami. 'Sit on that, you little yeller sub-human!'

'Can't,' Jap replied without rancour, 'got a double-decker bus up there already.'

But in spite of his need for a drink, the sergeant-despatcher appeared professional enough, as he opened the door and flooded the fuselage with icy cold air, before crying, 'Get ready!'

Obediently the officers and men of *Stormtroop Edelweiss* obeyed the command, struggling to their feet with their enormous loads of weapons and supplies.

The despatcher waited till they were in position. 'Hook up,' he commanded.

The snap of the metal catches being attached and

clicking into place could be heard the length of the plane, each man eyeing the life-giving catch to ensure that it was correctly fixed to the cable.

Again the despatcher waited. 'Check your equipment,' was his next order.

Just as they had been instructed back at Fuhlsbuttel, the troopers checked the connections of the man directly in front to ensure that all items were stowed away securely and would remain so when jarred by the tremendous opening shock of the chute.

Now that the little red light was winking off and on furiously like a baleful angry pink eye the men realized they were getting very close. Stuermer, in the number one position of the stick, could actually feel the plane sinking ever lower.

'Sound off for equipment check,' the despatcher called.

'*Number One – all right*,' Stuermer heard himself calling, as if from far away, his ears popping at the rapid change of altitude, his stomach descending deeper into his body, it seemed, as if on a fast lift.

'*Number Two – all right! . . . Number Three all right . . . Number Four . . .*' The barked replies ran the length of the plane till they reached the end of the stick, '*Number Sixteen – all right . . .*'

The despatcher looked at Stuermer, his eyes watery with drink, and some other emotion which the big mountain colonel could not define. 'Stand in the door!' he cried, above the wind which tore the words from his mouth, as he crouched there looking out for the dropping zone.

Weighed down by his load, Stuermer shuffled forward. Behind him the rest, their ashen faces clearly reflecting their fear at what was to come, did the same.

Stuermer balanced there, waiting for the command to jump. When it came, he knew, the whole stick would clear the Junkers in less then ten seconds. It would be the only way to keep together in that barren wild country below.

The seconds ticked past infinitely slowly like the last drops wrung from a drying well. Stuermer could feel the electric tingle of his over-excited nerves and the thump-thump of his heart pumping away like a trip-hammer. Below, the shadows of the three-engined transports swept across the snow like ghostly hands. He caught a glimpse of a patch of brown – birch trees, the silver gleam of a frozen lake, an area of naked rock surrounded by boulders. Then there it was – the dropping zone, a field of white, even snow, fringed by the peaks of the high plateau! Stuermer recognized it immediately, due to its triangular shape, from the aerial photographs he had been shown back in the Reich. This was it!

The despatcher's hand came down on Stuermer's shoulder. Hard. He did not hesitate. He knew he couldn't. The effect on the others would be disastrous. He launched himself into space, screaming like a crazy man.

Stuermer began to fall at a terrifying rate as the slipstream caught him. He was swirled round with the air roaring in his ears, deafening him, cruelly flattening his features, snatching the very air from his lungs so that he fought and choked for breath. *Would the parachute ever open?*

A sudden crack. A kind of sizzling sound as the rigging lines rushed upwards. Still he was falling at a tremendous speed. Instinctively Stuermer tensed his muscles for either the opening shock of the chute or that fatal impact with the ground at over 500 kilometres an hour. *Boom!* The chute flew open with a hellish, hollow boom. The opening shock of the canopy set off red and silver lights popping at the back of his eyeballs. A bag containing grenades was torn off by the impact and went whirling downwards, scattering its deadly eggs as it did so.

Gasping frantically for breath, Stuermer looked upwards. Above him the parachute had opened wide and fat and he suddenly felt small and insignificant beneath this gigantic white umbrella. Abruptly he was overcome by a sensation of lassitude, as he started to descend gently, the chute swinging softly from side to side, as if it were a garden swing and he was a small boy once again in short pants, wiling away a long lazy summer afternoon.

Down and down he came. Once he looked upwards and glimpsed the dark shapes of the Junkers overhead and the parachutes flowering like bubbles from a child's soap-pipe. Yet somehow they seemed so far away and to belong to another world, so he wasn't interested in the sight; all that concerned him was this joyous sensation of freedom and downright physical pleasure.

Stuermer's relaxed mood after the tension and the fear of the plane and the initial jump vanished almost as soon as it had come over him. For now, as he looked down, the snow-covered ground appeared to be racing up to meet him at a terrible rate. He tensed again, feeling every single muscle in his body go rigid. Desperately, he fought to relax. He knew that was vital, otherwise he could break a bone and that would be the end of him. Up here on the high plateau a broken leg or ankle meant almost certain death. He swallowed hard and managed to relax a little. He drew up his feet, both knees clasped tightly together as they had been told to do, his head bent slightly so that he wouldn't break his neck, if his head were jarred back violently on impact.

Now the ground was less than fifteen metres away. In a second he'd be down. He took a deep breath. The earth reached up and struck him a terrible blow in the feet. He could feel the jarring shock race right up through his legs, through his knees, to slap him sickeningly in the pit of the stomach. Instinctively he rolled to the right as they had been taught and slapped his whole length in the frozen snow. Next instant bright silver and red stars exploded in front of his eyes. A great black roaring set up in his ears. Something warm and salty trickled down his chin. Then he blacked out.

## SIX

General Dietl ducked hurriedly. Great brazen lights flickered evilly like the mouths of roaring blast furnaces glimpsed from afar. '*Hit the dirt!*' he cried urgently, as the morning air was ripped apart by an unholy, frightening howl. All around him, his staff officers, who had been standing on the quay surveying the entrance to the port of Narvik with their glasses, flung themselves onto the wet cobbles.

Not a moment too soon. Like the hush of a gigantic express train, the first shell from the ancient grey warship they had just sighted came hurtling towards the port. A thunderous roar. A tremendous smack. Beneath Dietl, the very earth trembled like a live thing and came up to slap him in the face. Acrid smoke assailed his nose and mouth until his lungs seemed about to burst. Desperately he fought for breath, as yet another monstrous shell from the English battleship hurtled down from the sky and smacked right into one of the tall silver-gleaming fish oil tanks. It began to burn immediately. Stinking cod-liver oil, a sea of blue flame, started to rush towards the docks.

Hierl, the general's personal aide, bleeding from a nasty wound in his temple, grabbed Dietl's arm. 'General,' he gasped, as red-hot gleaming slivers of shrapnel, some as big as a fist, howled through the air everywhere, 'we'd better get back to the command post, sir!'

Dietl swallowed hard. He had been under fire many a time before in World War One, but then he had been a younger man with better nerves. Now he could already begin to feel himself shaking, and it wouldn't do to let his men see the commanding general tremble. He nodded his head in agreement. 'Yes, you're right, Hierl, let's get the hell out of here! *Mir nach, Manner!*'

His staff officers needed no urging. Now the whole grey horizon was flickering a bright scarlet, as the British fleet off Narvik intensified their bombardment. They were in for a long and deadly barrage, they knew that; for today, on account of the low ceiling, their protecting Messerschmitts were unable to fly. They were practically defenceless against the British. Gripping their helmets like old women braving a high wind, the whole lot of them pelted after the commanding general into Narvik.

By this point the low roar of the British ships' bombardment had become a baleful angry scream, elemental but man-made and exact. Everywhere in the port the shells were bursting in a mighty anti-phonal crash. Dismembered bodies, German and Norwegian, flew in every direction, the burning ruins splashed an ugly blood-red. In the gutters, men and women writhed in their final agonies.

Dietl and his staff officers dashed from street to street, dodging falling masonry, showering down on all sides in a terrible fury of shattered timbers and broken bricks. A team of horses who had been pulling timber bolted past, eyes wild and wide with fright, their streaming manes already ablaze, scattering all before them. Red-hot shrapnel scythed the streets, howling off the walls and cutting soldier and civilian alike into a gory mess, so that the dismembered arms and legs looked like the bloody offal that butchers placed in front of the doors of their shops before the war, to be collected by the refuse-men. Dietl, his skinny chest heaving and gasping with the effort, took all this in and his confused, horrified brain told him that Narvik was about at the end of its tether. It would not survive much more of this kind of bombardment. He could see it, not only in the eyes of the panic-stricken Norwegian civilians cowering in the heaving, shaking doorways, but also in the gazes of his own men and writ large on their faces. The mountaineers' eyes were covered in a wet sheen, as if they might well break out into tears at any moment, and their lips were blue, twitching, and trembling uncontrollably.

Furiously, their heads bent, as if against heavy rain, arms working like pistons, the staff officers pelted towards the underground chamber below the town hall, which made up their command post; for here they had the advantage of the civilian telephone exchange, which still had not been cut off by the Norwegian forces to their south. Hierl screamed piteously like a wounded animal. Dietl flung a glance over his shoulder. His aide seemed to be leaning casually against the wall behind him, legs crossed. But his head was missing and blood was spurting up in a scarlet fountain from the severed neck! Dietl fought back the sickening hot bile which flooded his skinny throat and stumbled blindly inside the command post. Somehow or other he staggered down the steep steps leading to the bombproof underground chamber – how, he never knew later – and collapsed into his chair. Next moment his head fell into his hands and he began to sob piteously like a broken-hearted child, while his staff officers stared down at him helplessly, and the shelter rocked and heaved like a ship at sea caught in some monstrous tornado.

It was a good fifteen minutes before the general had recovered sufficiently to face up to the situation. By the time he became aware of his surroundings, a loud echoing silence had followed the initial British bombardment of the seaport. Awed, ashen-faced with shock, shaking their heads and wiping their faces clean of the grey cement dust, the staff officers waited for his decisions. In the room next to theirs, the telephones had already begun to shrill and excited voices were starting to repeat the hurried messages, as the clerks wrote them down. '*Eight destroyers sunk or beached . . . U-501 sinking rapidly in the shallows . . . all flak positions destroyed*' . . . and then the one message they had all dreaded to intercept: '*B-Service reports . . . British Admiral W. J. Whitworth recommending Admiralty, London . . . Narvik can be taken by direct assault without fear of meeting serious opposition on landing . . .*'

A staff officer caught his breath sharply. Another cursed, 'Holy strawsack, now the watch is really in the bucket!' Yet another took off his peaked cap and flung it furiously in the corner, face contorted with rage.

Dietl seemed curiously unaffected. When he spoke, his voice was toneless, very calm, almost too calm, as if he was in a state of shock. 'Well, *meine Herren*,' he said softly, as the telephones continued to jingle in the other room, 'there we have it. What we have been expecting for the last forty-eight hours is going to happen. The Tommies are coming – soon.' He stopped. Outside, the wall of a shell-shattered department store came tumbling down in a rush of masonry. When he spoke again, his voice had risen, grown in power and strength. 'I must tell you now, gentlemen, that I have the Führer's permission to withdraw the Mountain Division into neutral Sweden whenever I feel that to be necessary.'

There was an audible gasp of shock from the assembled staff officers, for they all knew what such a move would mean; they would be interned in Sweden until the war was over. Their army careers would be virtually ruined.

Dietl did not seem to hear the gasp. Instead he continued, voice calm, but yet firm and strong. 'I do not intend to avail myself of that order, gentlemen – *yet*. We shall stay here and fight for as long as we can. I know we are cut off save by air, the furthest German troops over five hundred kilometres to the south of Narvik. I know, too, that we have little more than machine guns to defend ourselves with against a tremendous weight of ships' artillery. But, gentlemen, we shall arm the crews of the sunken ships. I estimate that in this way we can about double our effectives.' For the first time since he had broken down after the enemy bombardment, Eduard Dietl's craggy, intelligent face broke into a wintry smile. 'We have one single ace up our sleeve.'

The staff officers stared at him, as if he were a conjuror about to produce a rabbit out of his top hat.

'Yes, Stuermer's *Stormtroop Edelweiss* is out there somewhere.' He made a vague gesture pointing to the east. 'I received a signal on the matter from the *OKW* just before the bombardment commenced.'

'*Stormtroop Edelweiss*,' the name went from mouth to mouth excitedly, and staff officers' wan, haggard faces lit up. They all knew of *Edelweiss*'s reputation. It was the elite of the elite.

'They are to protect our rear and deep right flank,' Dietl continued 'just in case the Tommies, instead of launching a direct assault on Narvik, attempt to nip us off in a pincer attack.'

The staff officers nodded their understanding and one of them asked eagerly, 'May I ask, sir, where they are located exactly?'

General Dietl's smile vanished instantly. He frowned and the worry was only too obvious in his red-rimmed tired eyes. '*Meine Herren*,' he announced, 'I am afraid I cannot tell you that. The pilots of the *Luftwaffe* Transport Command maintain that they dropped *Edelweiss* at the correct DZ[1] but that, due to low cloud and snow, they were unable to follow the rest of the drop.'

'In other words, sir,' the officer who had asked the original question said slowly, 'we don't know where *Stormtroop Edelweiss* is?'

Dietl nodded his head. 'I know Colonel Stuermer of old, gentlemen. He is one of the greatest climbers Germany has ever produced. He had lived in terrain that would have killed most of us within twenty-four hours. I am convinced he will get his command into

[1] Dropping zone.

position whatever the climatic and geographic difficulties. But all the same, I must emphasize this.' He stared around the circle of tired, haggard faces with his weary eyes. 'Since eleven hundred hours this morning, 13 April 1940, Stuermer and his men are posted officially "missing" . . .'

# SEVEN

*Ping! . . . Ping!*

The sharp crack of a rifle shattered the heavy brooding silence as a slug whined off one of the big boulders. Stone splinters showered the big man sprawled in the snow, his body muffled up by the collapsed canopy.

With a groan, Colonel Stuermer stirred. 'What was that?' he muttered, slowly opening his eyes and feeling the first sharp wave of red-hot pain spurt through his skull. With hands that felt as if they were clothed in thick boxing gloves, Stuermer found the release switch and opened it. Groaning once again, as his bruised head began to ache mercilessly, he crawled out of the canopy like a bug emerging out of its cocoon and knelt there in the frozen snow, wondering where he was and where the strange sound which had roused him had come from.

He stared about him. The vast sweep of snowfield, tinted pink from the blood-red ball of the sun which hung above the peaks, was empty. He was alone. The men who had dropped with him – how long ago, he couldn't know – had vanished, as if they had never even existed.

A sudden crack. As he ducked instinctively, he caught a glimpse of a faint puff of grey smoke coming from a group of snow-covered boulders two hundred metres or so to his right. He hit the snow face-first, headache forgotten now, as a bullet whistled just above his head and plunged into the snow with an angry hiss. He wasn't alone after all! There was somebody else out there and, whoever it was, it was certainly no friend of his. Or was it perhaps one of his missing troopers who had taken him for the enemy?

For what seemed an age, Stuermer crouched there, wondering what he should do, overcome at the same time by an uncanny eerie feeling that made the small hairs at the back of his head stand erect. Who in three devils' name could it be?

Suddenly he lost patience. He could already feel the icy cold creeping up his legs, stealing along a frozen path to his innards. He'd be in for a dose of frostbite if he didn't do something soon.

He cautiously raised himself and, cupping his hands about his mouth, yelled, 'Hello over there . . . This is Colonel St . . .'

The volley of quick fire drowned the rest of his words. Stuermer hit the snow fast, as half-a-dozen slugs bounced off the snow all around him.

He cursed and fumbled for the Schmeisser still strapped securely about his chest. At least, he knew now that whoever was out there was the enemy. Swiftly he made an assessment of his situation, as he freed the machine pistol and snapped off the safety catch, automatically checking that the long magazine was securely attached.

His only protection came from the fact that he had landed in a small depression, which was apparently 'dead ground' for whoever was shooting at him. Immediately he raised himself waist-high, he was a sitting duck. Desperately he cast around for some way out of the trap, some means of out-thinking his unknown enemy. He bit his bottom lip, mind racing furiously. Then he had it. Immediately ahead of him there was another boulder, perhaps some fifty metres away from his present position. Would his enemy expect him to make a dash for it and, if not, would he recover fast enough to shoot him down as he ran?

Stuermer swallowed hard. He knew there was no other way out. He had to find cover closer to the enemy in order to tackle him; otherwise he could well freeze to death in this merciless lunar landscape. He took a deep breath. '*One . . . two . . . three . . .*' he counted off the seconds to himself and then he was up and running for his very life, head tucked between his shoulders, zig-zagging violently to put the enemy off.

For a moment nothing happened. Then he heard a cry of rage. A dark, bearded face appeared from behind the boulders. There was the dull metal gleam of a rifle barrel. Stuermer tensed, desperately twisting to left and right to put the man off his aim.

In vain. Suddenly he felt a tremendous thump in his chest. He yelled out loud with the unbearable agony of it. The next instant he felt his legs giving beneath him, the whole front of his body afire with pain. Abruptly he sat down in the snow, staring numb and dazed at the Schmeisser which he had carried across his chest. It was completely smashed, the firing mechanism and magazine twisted grotesquely by the impact of the slugs at such close range. All the same, the little machine pistol had saved his life. '*But for how long?*' a malicious little voice at the back of his mind queried.

Stuermer felt for his knife. His only remaining weapon was gone! He had lost it from his jump-boot in his mad dash across the snow. He gasped with the shock of the discovery. He was weaponless, sprawled right out in the open. Was he fated to die worthlessly in this God forsaken place after all? Slowly, very slowly, he started to get to his feet, his hands rising in token of surrender.

'Hold it there, Fritz!' a gruff bass voice cried in rough German.

Stuermer froze.

A man was emerging from behind the rock where he had first seen the gunsmoke, a giant of a man, dressed in some huge fur that made him appear almost bearlike, with his beard and black fur cap. His rifle was pointed straight at Stuermer's heart and there was no mistaking the look of triumph and deadly intent on his rapacious face. Behind him a second man appeared, too, also armed, but smaller and dressed in what Stuermer took to be the uniform of the Royal Norwegian Army.

A flicker of hope flamed through Stuermer's mind. If

they were army men, he had a chance of being treated as a prisoner under the rules of the Geneva Convention. He relaxed a little.

The big bearlike Norwegian crooked a finger of his free hand at the prisoner, holding the heavy hunting rifle as if it were a child's toy. 'Come here, Fritz,' he said, his voice suddenly deceptively soft.

Alarm bells rang frantically in Stuermer's mind. He knew instinctively that the Norwegian was going to slaughter him in cold blood; he could see it in the shamefaced look of the smaller man. He felt the icy-cold sweat began to trickle down his spine unpleasantly. He forced himself to begin to move forward – to his death. Slowly, very slowly, as if savouring every second the Norwegian began to raise his rifle. By his side the other man said something sharply, then tried to grab the bearlike one's arm. Not even turning his head, the man with the rifle gave a slight push and the smaller one tumbled on his backside into the snow.

Stuermer continued to walk forward, automatically noting the Norwegian's knuckles whiten, as he took first pressure on the trigger. A second more and he, Stuermer, would be dead.

But that wasn't to be.

Two hundred metres away, the first figure in the familiar uniform of the *Edelweiss* appeared, silhouetted clearly against the white carpet of snow. Behind him others appeared. They stopped, as if puzzled by what was taking place below. Abruptly one of them fell to his right knee. His rifle flew up. Stuermer caught his breath. *Could he do it at that impossible range?*

The big Norwegian grinned, his mouth full of yellow teeth. 'So, Fritz,' he sneered. 'Now you know why you have come to Norway, eh?'

Stuermer tensed. This was it. The man who was going to kill him without mercy was taking second pressure. In an instant he would be dead, if . . .

'*To die*,' the Norwegian snarled through gritted teeth, eyes narrowed to evil black slits. 'Do you hear? To d . . .'

A single shot rang out. Dry and hard and clear like a twig being snapped underfoot in a hot summer. The Norwegian screamed. For a moment he teetered there, face wild with disbelief that this was happening to *him*. Slowly, infinitely slowly, the man lowered the rifle and deposited it almost gently on the snow. He sank to his knees, blood pouring from a great gaping wound in his back, his coat already wet and soaking with his life fluid. For an age, he seemed to crouch there, shaking his shaggy head like an animal, trying to fight off death, growling through clenched teeth, the snow all around him covered with bright-red gobs of blood. Suddenly he threw back his head in one last unbearable paroxysm of agony and howled at the sky. Next moment he had plunged face forward into the snow, dead . . .

'Thank God, sir . . . thank God!' Greul gasped, dropping his rifle and patting Stuermer's chest, as if he had half-expected to find some terrible wound beneath the shattered Schmeisser.

'No, thank *you* and your keen eyesight,' Stuermer said with more gaiety than he felt at that moment, 'or otherwise that animal over there might well have been having me for his supper this day.'

A little way off, Ox-Jo contemptuously turned over the giant with the toe of his boot, while at his side the Norwegian soldier, if that was what he was, cowered on his knees, babbling incoherently to himself, hands clasped together in the classical pose of supplication.

'Dead as doornail,' Ox-Jo announced. 'You put the bullet right through his ugly big turnip, Major.' He let the Norwegian fall back on his face again, thankfully hiding the livid contorted face with a great ragged gory hole now where the right eye had been, from view.

'What's the situation?' Stuermer pulled himself

together and, whipping the ruined Schmeisser over his head, noted that Greul had collected about half *Stormtroop Edelweiss*. 'Where are the others? Many casualties?'

Greul, as always, was efficiency itself. Clicking to attention, he reported as if he were back on the parade ground at Kufstein. 'Sixty men missing, sir . . . One man dead on landing, two left back over there with assorted broken limbs.'

Stuermer sucked his teeth hard. Fifty per cent of his command missing, without a single shot having been fired. 'I see,' he said, trying to keep his voice non-committal for the sake of the men. 'I'm sure they'll turn up in due course. The sticks just got scattered, that's all. We'd better build some sort of recognition beacon so that they can orientate themselves on it. Ox, you and that disgraceful little friend of yours, Jap, shin up that peak up there and raise the *Edelweiss* standard.'

Ox-Jo grinned and nudged Jap, who was chewing aimlessly on a piece of hard salami. 'Come on, arse-with-ears. Don't stand there with yer tail hanging out of yer trap. You heard the CO. Let's make steam!'

Obediently, Jap 'made steam'.

Stuermer turned to Greul again. 'Contact with the enemy, Major?' he queried.

Greul's face hardened. 'I don't know rightly, sir,' he said hesitantly. 'I have a feeling that there is someone here,' he indicated the dead man and their trembling prisoner. 'Obviously. We also spotted a lot of footprints back there in the snow, perhaps half an hour from here, but as far as actual contact goes . . .' he shrugged uncertainly and left the rest of his sentence unfinished.

Stuermer nodded his understanding and involuntarily cast a nervous glance over his shoulder, as if he half expected to see the whole of the Norwegian Army advancing upon them. But the ice waste was empty, save for the wind stirring up the loose surface snow into softly dancing 'ice-devils'. He frowned and nodded to the man on his knees. 'I think, Greul, we'd better have a look-see at that particularly unhappy specimen of Norwegian manhood.'

Greul barked an order and one of the corporals, a big happy-go-lucky mountain-farmer from the Bavarian Alps, who couldn't seem to get used to army discipline, put the toe of his mountain boot underneath the Norwegian's bottom, growling in his thick accent, which even Stuermer found difficult to understand, 'Get up you sow! The Gentleman Colonel wants to speak with you. *Los!*'

Trembling like a leaf, tears streaming down his frozen face, the Norwegian soldier stumbled forward.

Stuermer kept his voice deliberately low. When interrogating a prisoner, he knew it was no use attempting to frighten him until the occasion called for it. 'Sweet and sour,' he called the technique – like Chink food. First the promises and then the threats. Besides, the wretch had attempted to save his life.

'Do you speak German?' he asked softly.

The man nodded his head, as if he didn't trust himself to speak.

'What is your unit?' Stuermer continued, taking it step by step, though a little voice at the back of his mind cautioned urgency; there was trouble, serious trouble, not far off.

The Norwegian licked cracked, parched lips uneasily. Finally he spoke. 'First Battalion, the Telemark Regiment.'

Stuermer thought quickly, trying to visualize the situation map he had last seen at Fuhlsbuttel. It was always good to dominate a prisoner by impressing upon him the depth of one's own knowledge of the enemy dispositions. 'At Kristiansand under the command of Major-General Liljedal.'

The prisoner was suitably impressed. 'Yes, Kristiansand on the coast,' he agreed eagerly.

'And what are you doing here? It's a long way to Kristiansand.'

The prisoner hesitated.

Stuermer frowned deliberately. 'Well,' he barked in his best Prussian tone, 'out with it, man!'

'Sir, I can't . . .'

'Don't play games with me,' Stuermer interrupted him brutally, playing the 'sour' role now. He nodded to the grinning ex-farmer who cottoned on immediately, deliberately slipping off the safety catch on his rifle and tugging back the bolt.

The Norwegian paled. His whole body shook with fear. 'Sir,' he pleaded, clasping his hands together once more in dire appeal, 'please don't shoot me . . . I'm just an ordinary man. I do as I am ordered. *Bitte, bitte, nicht scheissen* . . .' His face was contorted with agony. '*Nicht Scheissen!*'

Under normal circumstances, Stuermer would have laughed out loud. The poor fellow had confused the German word for 'shit' with that for 'shoot'.[1] But he knew he had to appear to be hard and resolute to get what he wanted to know out of him. 'Then speak,' he commanded fiercely, eyes gleaming, 'or else . . .'

That did the trick. The man stuttered, 'Most of the regiment surrendered, sir. But the men of the First Battalion decided to fight on . . . We retreated up here all yesterday and then we made contact with the – er, er—' he obviously sought for the word in German and then he had it, 'the Wild Ones.'

'The Wild Ones?' Stuermer echoed. 'What in three devils' name are they, man?'

'The Wild Ones, why, sir they are—'

The hoarse stutter of an ancient machine gun like the angry chatter of a frustrated woodpecker broke into his explanation. Next to the prisoner, Stuermer saw the corporal clawing the air as if climbing the rungs of an invisible ladder. The prisoner stared at him in amazement until his face, too, creased with an unbearable agony. Abruptly what looked like red-buttonholes appeared the length of his skinny chest. He fell without another word.

[1] Sch*ei*ssen – shit; Sch*ie*ssen – shoot.

'They're coming . . . they're coming, sir . . . dozens of the bastards!'

Ox-Jo's mighty voice alerted him to the new danger and even as he started to bellow out his orders to the *Edelweiss* troopers hitting the snow everywhere, Colonel Stuermer knew with a sinking feeling that the balloon had gone up. They were under attack again . . .

# *BOOK TWO: DEATH ON THE HIGH PLATEAU*

# ONE

'Hit the deck, you great horned-ox!' Jap hissed urgently, as the ragged firing broke out everywhere below in the valley. He hastily gave his big companion, standing there startled and open-mouthed, a hefty push so that Ox-Jo tumbled to the snow, followed a moment later by his smaller comrade. 'And for Chrissake, suck in that monstrous fart-cannon of yourn,' he added breathlessly. 'It can be seen a shitting kilometre away at least!'

Ox-Jo hurriedly tucked in his buttocks and stared with growing apprehension at what was taking place below.

Colonel Stuermer and the rest of the *Stormtroop* had been caught completely off guard. Now they were trapped in a small hollow, which protected them as long as they hugged the dead ground, bodies clasped to the snow, as if in an embrace with a hot, juicy *fraulein*; while all around them little groups of men, some dressed in the shaggy black furs similar to those worn by the lone man they had killed, some in the khaki of the Norwegian Army, poured a concentrated hail of rifle fire onto their positions.

'Great shit on the shingle,' Jap cursed unhappily, as they watched from their hiding place, 'they've really gone and caught the CO with his knickers round his ankles this time!'

Ox-Jo nodded glumly as he slipped off the safety catch of his machine pistol, a look of grim determination settling onto his big red face. 'Treacherous bastards,' he grunted through gritted teeth, 'why don't they shitting well admit that we've gone and done them the shitting favour of occupying their shitting miserable country and shitting well give in? Now they've sneaked up on us like that. It ain't shitting well,' he tightened his grip on the

Schmeisser, which looked like a child's toy gun in his massive paw, '*fair!* But I'll show . . .'

Jap grabbed him just in time. 'Get down, you silly fart-in-a-trace!' he yelled hastily. 'What the shit do you think you're gonna be able to do down there on yer lonesome? There must be,' he did a quick count, 'a good two hundred of the limp-pricks down there!'

Ox-Jo bit his lip and relaxed. 'Yer right, you little-arse-with-plush-ears, I suppose,' he admitted grudgingly, lowering his Schmeisser. 'But we can't let them go and croak the CO and the lads without doing shitting anything, Jap. Holy strawsack, we can't let that happen!'

Jap, his cunning little Asiatic brain racing, wildly sought for a way out of the mess. He knew nothing much could happen to them all as long as Colonel Stuermer just kept the boys in position down there, with their turnips well tucked in. Naturally, as soon as the light started to go, the Norwegians would begin to infiltrate *Stormtroop*'s positions. But the sun, blood-red and sinister, was still high in the heavens. There was time enough *yet.*

'Listen, Ox,' he said, his voice urgent with all the usual banter gone, 'the CO sent us out to signal to the rest of the *Stormtroop*. Now instead of signalling for them so that they walk straight into the trap, too, we go out and *find* them. Colonel Stuermer estimates that there must be at least another fifty of the boys out there. With that number we could give those Norwegians a very nasty surprise.'

Ox-Jo's big face lit up. 'Right in one, in the shape of a very sharp bayonet up their fat Nor . . .' He broke off suddenly, gaze focused on something just behind Jap's head.

'What is it?' Jap hissed, instinctively keeping his voice low.

'Two of them,' Ox-Jo whispered, holding his mouth close to Jap's ear, but not taking his gaze off the men he had just spotted, both dressed in the same shaggy furs as the one they had killed. 'They haven't seen us. They're settling down up there. Perhaps they're some kind of rearguard. Take a peek.'

Cautiously, hardly daring to breathe, Jap craned his head round. Ox-Jo was right. Two hefty men, made even larger by their fur coats, were squatting among the rocks only fifty metres away, apparently eating, their rifles cradled in the crook of their free arms. 'Shit on the shingle!' he hissed angrily, 'that's crapped on things. We can't get over the rise without them spotting us, Ox.'

'Yer don't have to draw me a picture,' he said with suppressed anger. 'There's no other way for it, Jap. We've got to nobble those two.' He lowered his Schmeisser softly to the snow, 'And this is the way we've gonna have to do it.' He held up one big paw like a small steam shovel. 'If we used the popguns, the other shits down there would hear.'

Jap bit his lip. The two men crouched eating in the snow were big, very big. Ox-Jo would be able to manage his all right, but if he, Jap, didn't achieve surprise and the Norwegian got a good grip on him – He decided not to think that particularly unpleasant thought through. Instead he said urgently, 'All right, Ox, I'm on. You take the one to the right of the boulder, I'll nobble the arsehole to the left.' Hastily he unslung his own Schmeisser and placed it on the snow, wetting his suddenly parched lips and opening his mouth to test the wind. The moisture on his lips dried immediately as he turned in the direction of the enemy. 'The wind's coming from their direction,' he hissed.

In spite of his tension, Ox-Jo grinned in admiration. His little yellow-faced wizened running-mate had a lot of his Hunza ancestors in him; he knew tricks that he, Ox-Jo, had never even dreamed about. Affectionately, he patted the smaller man's shoulder. 'All right, apeturd, off we go – and look after yourself.'

'You, too, you Bavarian barnshitter,' Jap replie[illegible] emotion in his voice not altogether concealed.

They spread out, crouched low in the snow,

almost imperceptibly with all the skills they had learned in months of training in the high mountains, making hardly a sound. Fortunately the faint warmth of the sun had melted the top surface of the frozen snow and made their progress almost noiseless. The light wind did the rest.

Now Jap could make out the details of his opponent more clearly. He really was a giant, he told himself with a sinking feeling, as he crawled ever closer, dark Oriental eyes fixed almost hypnotically on the man's massive back, above which a thick red bull-neck was surmounted by a great ragged thatch of jet-black hair. Jap could even smell the man now. He had a particularly rancid smell, composed not only of animal and human sweat, but also of raw meat, that of wild animals; and judging by the way the Norwegian was gnawing pleasurably at the hunk of meat he held in his right hand, Jap guessed that he ate a great deal of it. The knowledge increased his feeling of anxiety. His opponent-to-be was a man of the wilds, a hunter perhaps, who would know how to take care of himself in the toughest of situations. He would be no push-over. He had to get in the first blow – 'and make it, do you hear, *make it sit!*' a harsh, angry little voice demanded at the back of his mind.

Jap nodded in grim agreement and crawled on.

Now he and Ox-Jo, some twenty metres away, were almost on the two Norwegians, who conversed in guttural monosyllables in between gnawing noisily at their meat, making little pleasurable sounds when they found a particularly tasty bit, pausing only to wipe the grease and blood from their bearded chins with the backs of the hands. Jap flashed a look at Ox-Jo.

The latter nodded back, his face set and tense. Slowly, very slowly, he held up his right hand and flashed the fingers up and down twice.

Jap knew what he meant. In ten seconds he would go in for the attack. He began to crawl on, hardly daring to breathe now.

Confidently, Ox-Jo raised himself. He knew that there were very few men in this world who could beat him in a fair fight. He was a match for most men. But he was worried that Jap wouldn't be able to tackle the other giant, for the man was – at a hasty assessment – at least forty pounds heavier than the skinny, undersized half-breed. He, Ox-Jo, would have to get in there quick, nobble his own Norwegian, then be ready to help Jap if he got into trouble. He drew a deep breath, nostrils wrinkling in disgust as they were assailed by the stench coming from his victim. 'Christ,' he told himself, 'he smells like a goddam gorrilla's armpit!' Then he closed his mouth firmly, flung one last glance at Jap, who seemed to be fumbling for something in the snow, and dived forward.

He hit the Norwegian with all of his two hundred pounds of brawn and hard muscle. The man gasped with shock. The hunk of half-raw meat flew from his hairy paw. He tried to turn round. Ox-Jo didn't give him a chance. 'Try this on for size, *stinkarse!*' he roared and crooked a brawny arm around the man's bearded throat. The yell he was about to make was cut off immediately, as Ox-Jo flexed the muscles that threatened to burst out of his sleeve at any moment, and exerted pressure.

In vain the Norwegian grabbed at Ox-Jo's arm. His body arched and he began to make little wheedling, gasping sounds, eyes frantic as he tried to break that murderous hold. Ox-Jo grunted, his own face crimson with effort, sweat dripping from his brow in spite of the freezing cold, as he laid on more pressure. The Norwegian tried to bend down and bite at Ox-Jo's fingers clenched under his Adam's apple. Ox-Jo reacted instinctively. He thrust his thumb up. It went easily into the Norwegian's left nostril and Ox-Jo ripped up and outwards, still maintaining his killing hold. The Norwegian's whole body shook under the almost unbearable pain. For one lo horrible moment, as the hot blood ran down his knu Ox-Jo thought he was going to lose him. But som managed to hang on. Now he brought up his right knee, carefully, deliberately. It seemed to take him a long time to find the correct spot in the Norwegian's heaving back. Then he had it. He pressed the knee home. With another grunt, while the Norwegian writhed and twisted frantically, trying to break that deadly hold, he rammed the knee even deeper into his back and, the sweat running down his brick-red face in rivulets, making it gleam as if greased with vaseline, he began to exert the final pressure. Then and only then, did he dare cast a look at his little running-mate, Jap.

Jap's Norwegian lay on the snow, vomit spilling from his mouth onto the snow, great lumps of half-raw dark-red meat, his fingers clawing at the stuff, while Jap systematically battered-in the back of his skull with the rock he had found at the very last moment.

It was an appalling scene. Jap was murdering his Norwegian in cold blood in the cruellest of ways. All the same, his heart leapt with admiration at the cunning of his little companion. Jap had found his equalizer – the rock – and had used it in the fiendishly clever manner of his half-wild Hunza ancestors. Then he turned away, sickened by what was happening over there, as Jap clubbed his rock down on the man's shattered skull once again, like a workman bringing down a heavy steel hammer, and the blood spurted in bright gleaming jets from the dying Norwegian's nose and ears.

Grimly, he concentrated on finishing off his own victim. '*Die, you stinking shit!*' he cursed through gritted teeth, as the man's fingers clawed feebly at his battered, bloody hands, strange, weird whimpering noises coming from down deep in his windpipe. '*For fuck's sake* – DIE!'

The Norwegian seemed to take an incredibly long time to do so. His eyes popped out of his head, wild and wide with agony. His tongue hung out of his gaping, gasping mouth like a purple tag, while he pounded the snow with his right hand weakly, like a spoilt petulant child having a temper tantrum because he wasn't getting his way.

Ox-Jo exerted every last bit of strength in his massive body, the muscles creaking with the effort, his broad back aflame, top teeth biting into his bottom lip until his mouth was flooded with hot salty blood. That did it. Suddenly the Norwegian arched. Ox-Jo almost lost him. A strange rattle came down within his ruptured throat. Ox-Jo sighed with heartfelt relief. He had done it! He gave one more squeeze to make quite sure and looked down at the Norwegian's face cradled in his brawny arms. But his victim's eyes were wide, bulging, staring into nothing. He was dead all right. With a sudden feeling of revulsion, absolute and complete disgust, he flung the man he had murdered away from him – he slumped to the ground like a broken doll. An instant later Ox-Jo followed him, sinking to his haunches, his breath coming in violent hectic gasps, his every limb trembling, as he fought off the nausea that threatened to overwhelm him . . .

'I'll get the mps,'[1] Jap said tonelessly, finally breaking the heavy silence, punctuated only by the occasional rattle of rifle-fire below.

'*Gut*. I'll strip,' Ox-Jo didn't complete the sentence with 'bodies'. 'We can use those fur coats.'

Jap nodded and headed down the slope to where they had left their Schmeissers.

Reluctantly, nose wrinkled in distaste, Ox-Jo started to strip the heavy fur coats off the men they had just killed so cruelly. The fur was dark and shaggy and smelled of the dead animal to which it had once belonged, the pelt inside poorly tanned so that it was still greasy, as if rubbed in beast-fat. 'Wolf,' Jap said, returning and putting Ox-Jo's Schmeisser on the ground. 'They must have been some kind of hunters, I suppose.'

'Real hairy-assed old bastards, the two of 'em,' Ox-Jo declared, finally completing the unpleasant task. 'They might even have a flatman with them, but I don't think

[1] Machine pistols.

I'd want to drink any kind of sauce those dirty bastards had.'

'Yer right there, Ox,' Jap agreed, wiping away the last of the dried blood from where it had congealed between his fingers. 'I've smelt better cat's piss than the pong those shits give off. Christ Almighty, I'll bet they ain't had a wash since the day they were born!'

'Might be,' Ox-Jo said, slipping on the greatcoat with a barely concealed shudder, noting that the sun had virtually disappeared now and that the sky was turning a leaden, ominous grey. 'But let's be on our way. Time's running out.'

Jap nodded his agreement and flashed a look down below. The firing had almost ceased. The attackers seemed in no hurry to launch an all-out attack, and Jap knew why. There was snow on the way and, in the kind of blizzard that raged up here on the high plateau, the Norwegians would be inside Colonel Stuermer's positions before the CO knew what had hit him. He grabbed the other coat, his repulsion at the stench forgotten now. 'Yer, let's make steam, Ox, before it's too late.'

Five minutes later they had disappeared over the crest of the ridge into the snow-heavy birches beyond. Behind them, the first sad flakes started to drift down aimlessly . . .

# TWO

'With all due respect, sir,' the tall handsome major in the red and white checked cap of the Scots Guards bellowed above the wind and the thunder of the *Warspite*'s 15-inch guns, '*do we or don't we?*' He flashed a quick look at the coast, already rapidly disappearing into thick yellow smoke, as the *Warspite*'s great shells ripped the German positions there apart.

The general frowned hesitantly. For twenty-four hours now the War Office and the First Lord, Churchill, had been urging him to take action against Narvik. The time of decision had arrived and it was damnably difficult. Dare he risk the lives of the four thousand odd men of his brigade in such a chancy venture, especially when most of them were untrained Reservists, or Territorials called up the previous September?

Major, The Laird of the Seven Lochs, Rory Ferguson, once known to his fellow Guardees of the Guards Club as 'Red Rory' on account of his flaming red hair, or more bitterly because of his title and arrogance, 'The Man Who Walks Over Water', understood the fat middle-aged general's hesitancy. He hadn't seen action since 1918. Since then, working his slow way up the ladder of promotion, the only decisions he had been called to make in the peacetime Regular Army were what colour were the men to blanco their equipment or whether he should give some unfortunate soldier seven or fourteen days 'jankers' because he lacked the regulation thirteen studs in the sole of his ammunition boots. All the same, Red Rory had no tolerance of his hesitancy. He had been in action ever since he had seconded from the brigade for the hard, bitter fighting of the North-West Frontier in 1937, followed by the same kind of irregular warfare in

Palestine in 1939. He knew from past experience that the general who hesitates when the right moment has come, fails. Now the right moment had arrived and still the brigade commander wasn't certain.

'Sir,' he tried again, 'I know the prospect seems daunting, with the Hun dug in over there and a couple of hundred miles of pretty rough terrain to cross before we can link up with the Norwegians on the High Plateau, but his coastal defences must be stretched so much that he can't have more than a platoon to stop us out there and I've got a reinforced company, two hundred men. And I'm pretty sure my chaps can take the terrain.'

The general looked at the Guards major as if seeing him for the first time, noting the bronzed, tough face with the customary trim moustache, the broad chest decorated with the purple and white ribbon of the Military Cross, and then flashed a glance at his Guardsmen, waiting on the deck beyond, all of them dressed as if they were about to go on parade at Buckingham Palace. 'You might be right, Major,' he said, his voice weary and strained, 'but can your chaps stand the strain? I mean they're all Reservists, called back to the colours, after God only knows how many years in civvy street. They're probably quite soft by now and the terrain and climate up there will be murderous, so Intelligence says.'

'They'll stand the strain, sir, rest assured of that,' Red Rory said quietly. 'After all they *are* Guardsmen!'

The general sucked the end of his straggly, old-fashioned moustache, dating back to the days when he too had been a dashing young major of the line in 1918, sporting his new purple and white ribbon proudly. 'Hm,' he grunted, 'it is not merely a matter of committing your chaps, Ferguson. It's the rest of the brigade, four thousand men and all of them – Terriers! Weekend soldiers, with more training in supping beer in the drill hall than in weapon handling.'

'But, sir,' Red Rory persisted, 'if we can make the link-up with the Norwegians, get them properly organized so that we can roll up the Hun's flank, he'll simply have to abandon Narvik or be completely cut off. *Then*, it should be a walkover for the brigade, sir. Your Terriers can march in without having fired a shot, their rifles at the slope, as if it were Empire Sunday and the kids were waving flags at them.' He paused for breath, his chest heaving with the effort of talking so much, his light blue, bold eyes flashing fire.

The general looked at the coast, now almost completely obscured by thick yellow gunsmoke, then back to the tall Guards major's excited young face, remembering the day back in 1918 when he had talked *his* brigadier into holding the line of the canal against the weight of the surprise German attack on Gough's Fifth Army, and had thus saved the brigade from being overwhelmed, and said, 'All right then, hang it. Off you go, Major Ferguson!'

Red Rory grinned, saluted, and not giving his commander a chance to change his mind again, turned and yelled to Sergeant-Major MacDonald, one of the few regulars in his company, 'All right, Sarnt-Major, get them in the boats, we're off!'

MacDonald, nearly seven feet tall and broad with it, swung his CO a tremendous, hand-quivering salute and bellowed above the roar of the guns, 'All right, me lucky lads, the CO's gone and got yer a battle. Get into them boats, *gildy!*' In spite of his name, his accent was pure East End Cockney. His waxed moustache trembled, as he added, 'And woe betide anyone of you pregnant penguins who drops his rifle into the drink. His feet won't touch the ground till he reaches the glasshouse. Now over the side!'

The big Guardsmen, laden with battle-kit and gas-masks, rifles and bren-guns slung over their shoulders, began to go over the side, clinging anxiously to the rope netting, trying to judge the distance between the sides of the troopship and boats below and pick the right moment to drop down. Above them the Territorials began to cheer. Somebody bawled out a chorus of, '*We're gonna hang out the washing on the Siegfried Line . . . have yer any dirty washing, mother dear . . .*' A destroyer tore across the front, a white bone in its teeth, its siren hooting as it started to spread a thick black smokescreen to cover the landing. With unusual formality, the general clicked to attention and saluted.

Red Rory swallowed his gasp of amazement. It was as if the Old Man was bidding them good-bye for ever. He grinned hard and returned the salute in the slow arrogant way of the Brigade of Guards and called above the sudden racket, 'See you soon, sir – *in Narvik!*' Then, grasping his precious Tommy-gun more tightly in his big, capable hand, he too was over the net and scrambling his precarious way down to the swaying, bobbing boats far below.

The general sighed and sucked the end of his straggly moustache in that strange adolescent manner of his. 'I wonder,' he began, speaking to himself in the fashion of the lonely man that he was, then stopped. Instinctively he knew he would never see the handsome young Guards officer again. But now it was too late for second thoughts. The invasion of Norway had commenced . . .

The climb up the cliff under the cover of the smoke had been hell. Laden with nearly sixty pounds of kit, the Guardsmen had sweated and cursed their way upwards, delayed time and time again by the cunningly constructed wire ledges that the German defenders had placed there to stop an ascent such as theirs. Sucking his lacerated hands, the Laird had sworn eternal perdition to the War Office more than once for having sent them to Norway so ill-prepared; there hadn't been one single pair of wire cutters in the whole of the brigade! But now they hugged the top of the cliff, breathing leathern-lunged with the effort, their faces lathered in sweat in spite of the icy wind.

Red Rory wiped the blood off his hands on the white, frozen grass and peered through the drifting smoke at what lay ahead. Somewhere down there to the right was

Narvik. He could tell its position from the scarlet spurts of flame from the German guns. To his left was the rocky trail, flecked here and there with patches of dirty frozen snow, that led from the port out and up towards the High Plateau. Just there, where it branched off from the road that ran along the coast, he was sure they would find the Huns. He focused his glasses more accurately while, beside him, big Sergeant-Major MacDonald waited tensely for his decision, his keen, dark eyes flashing to left and right and taking in the Guardsmen sprawled in the sparse grass, rifles at their shoulders, their bodies twisted at the regulation forty-five degree angle as they had been taught to do by the musketry sergeant back at Pirbright. The Jocks were a bit soft after civvy street, he told himself approvingly, but a few days in the mountains would run the flab off them, and then they'd show the Jerries, just as their fathers had done back in the Old War. The Jocks, he knew instinctively, wouldn't let him or the CO down. Cor, stone the ferking crows, they were more scared of him than the whole ruddy ferking Jerry army!

A low, rough stone building, roofed by cast-iron sheeting, glittering with frost, swung into the calibrated glass circles of Red Rory's binoculars. It was just off the crossroads, the sort of place that lazy or inexperienced soldiers would make for to set up their headquarters, not realizing that it made an ideal target for enemy artillery. Were the Germans like that? He observed the place closely. There was a faint trickle of lazy grey smoke coming from the chimney, but that meant nothing. Peasants might be occupying the place. Suddenly his heart stopped beating for a moment. He was right. A tall skinny fellow in field-grey with a kind of ski cap set at a jaunty angle came out of the door – and he was carrying a rifle over his shoulder. Red Rory dropped his glasses at once. Only Germans would be carrying rifles in this part of Norway. 'Sarnt-Major,' he snapped urgently.

MacDonald forgot the irritating fact that Duncan, 175,

was lacking a stud in his right boot and that, really, he should put the sandy-haired Guardsman on a 'fizzer' for being idle and sloppy to that extent. 'Sir,' he barked.

'Keep it down to quiet roar,' Red Rory curbed his sergeant-major's majestic parade-ground voice, '*please* . . . They're in that hut, or around it. They're pretty thin on the ground, as we suspected, so they're simply guarding the crossroads,' he lied hopefully.

'I see, sir. And the drill?'

'We go in from the flanks. You take half the company, I'll take the other. No heroics please. This isn't the Charge of the Light Brigade. I want as few casualties as possible. Get in as close as you can, then make out as if the whole Brigade of Guards is coming in with bayonets – no unnecessary firing. I don't want us to start shooting each other up. Got it?'

'*Got it!*' MacDonald rasped, feeling his blood racing, as the adrenaline began to pump thick and fast. It was the same feeling that he had experienced in the old days when he had been a mere Guardsman, with no responsibilities, and they'd gone 'civvy-bashing' on Saturday evenings after the boozers had turned out.

Hastily, Red Rory rose to his knees and snapped, 'All right, you chaps, listen to me. This is what we're going to do.' In a few sentences he explained to his men how they were going to do it, adding that simple command which sent a sudden shiver of apprehension down the spines of the most case-hardened of the big men, '*Fix bayonets!* And, oh, yes,' he commanded, 'throw away those damned gasmasks. Nobody can fight with those bloody things choking you!'

Obediently, the men started to pull off the square khaki-coloured packs attached to their chests, while Sergeant-Major MacDonald looked worried. What kind of CO was it who told his men to throw away War Department property that had been officially accounted and signed for? He must be a rum'un!

*

'Freeze!' Red Rory commanded.

'What is it, sir?' the sergeant crawling behind him asked.

'Wire,' Red Rory replied shortly. Now they were only a hundred yards from the little shack guarding the crossroads.

'We didna have cutters,' the NCO interjected.

'You don't have to tell me that, Sergeant,' Red Rory answered, trying to keep his temper. Every minute they wasted spelled danger; the Huns sheltering in the hut against the raw wind might just look out and then they'd be up the creek without a paddle. The place had damned stout walls, proof against anything they could fire at them. 'Cairn and O'Brian!' he shouted.

'Sir.'

'Lift the sod the best you can so that the rest of us can squeeze through. Use your handkerchiefs to protect your hands if you can.'

The two Guardsmen squirmed forward, turned on their backs and pushed upwards with all their strength, wincing with pain as the cruel barbs cut into their palms. 'Ye can come nu, sir,' Cairn gasped.

Red Rory did not hesitate. 'After me,' he commanded and squeezed under the wire. One by one his men followed him swiftly. 'Spread out,' he muttered softly. Obediently, the Guardsmen did so, big bodies tensed, as they stole forward, rifles clutched tightly to their sides, breath fogging on the icy air.

Now they were only fifty yards away from the place. Red Rory, Tommy-gun cradled in his hands, could see its every detail clearly. They were going to do it; they were going to surprise the Germans.

But that wasn't to be.

Suddenly the door opened with a rusty squeak. It was almost like the sound doors made in the ghost films that Red Rory had so enjoyed in his youth. A tall, skinny German stood there, his jacket already open, braces dangling, with a sheet of newspaper in his hands. It was all too obvious what he was in the process of doing. He stopped abruptly, mouth hanging open stupidly, as he stared in disbelief at the hundred or so big men who stood staring back at him. Slowly, very slowly, as if they were watching a badly made film, the Guardsmen watched the German start to open his mouth.

Red Rory didn't wait for him to shout. He raised the Tommy-gun and fired without aiming. The chatter shattered the heavy stillness. The German screamed, reeling back to slam against the stone wall, what looked like a series of red button holes stitched the length of his chest. In the same instant that the Guardsmen charged, he slithered to the ground dead.

Suddenly violence erupted everywhere. A heavy machine gun chattered to the right. Tracer flew towards the running men. Red Rory cursed. He had overlooked the machine gun, cunningly concealed in a patch of scrub to the right of the house. Next to him, a Guardsman spun round under the impact of a salvo of bullets at such short range and fell to the ground, his body smoking with the tracer. Another sank to the snow, nursing an abruptly shattered knee, staring at his ruined leg and sobbing heart-brokenly.

Red Rory's face hardened as he dashed forward, firing from the hip as he did so, blue angry sparks erupting from the building's stone walls, as the line of slugs hurried towards the only window. Now his Guardsmen were finding out what real war was all about. It had nothing to do with bullshitting their boots, blancoing their equipment and brushing their bearskins. This was the real thing where men screamed in pain and stared at shattered knees, as if they couldn't believe it was happening to them.

'At the double, you 'orrible men – give 'em the sodding point!' Sergeant-Major MacDonald's tremendous voice came floating in from the other flank. Abruptly the chatter of the German machine gun stuttered to a stop and Red Rory told himself MacDonald had seen them off.

A German in a peaked cap came running round the side of the house. Red Rory swung from the hip and the man skidded to a stop, all flailing arms and legs. His rifle clattered to the ground and he sank to his knees. As he ran by the dying German, Red Rory lashed out with his steel-tipped boot. The man's head shot back, his neck broken. he fell forward on his shattered face, the splintered bones gleaming a brilliant white in the sudden red gore.

Another German, young but determined, the gleam of fanaticism set on his handsome face, raced at Red Rory, bayonet fixed. He swung round, Tommy-gun at the ready, and pressed the trigger. Nothing happened! The German screamed exultantly and came in for the kill. Red Rory tensed. He could almost feel that long, gleaming, deadly-sharp bayonet sliding red-hot into his guts.

Next moment Sergeant-Major MacDonald loomed up out of the fog of war. 'You naughty man!' he bellowed, as if he were reprimanding some unfortunate Guardsman back at Pirbright for having a tunic button undone. His bayonet slashed forward. The German parried, but he didn't stand a chance against the giant NCO who had been teaching recruits bayonet drill when he had still been in short pants. MacDonald thrust his rifle to the right. Their blades clanged together. MacDonald heaved. Red Rory could see those brutal shoulder muscles bulge against the tight serge. Next moment, the big NCO brought up his brass-shot butt and rammed it right into the German's chin. He went reeling back, spitting blood and broken teeth, his rifle falling from nerveless fingers. MacDonald towered above the German sprawled there on the ground, bayonet upraised, but then slowly, almost reluctantly, he lowered his bayonet. The German could have been his own son, at present back in the training depot at Caterham. He couldn't kill the kid in cold blood. 'All right, you,' he barked, 'tell the others to come out camerading – *schnell . . . schnell*, right smartish, do you hear?' The unfamiliar words came back to him as if from another era when he, too, had been a sixteen-year-old volunteer who had lied about his age so that he could escape the crippling poverty of the Mile End Road for the trenches.

The boy understood. Holding his shattered jaw, he called awkwardly, '*Nicht scheissen, Kameraden . . . Die Tommies wollen, dass wir uns ergeben . . . Schluss machen . . .*'

Red Rory frowned as the Germans, half a dozen of them, tanned faces suddenly pale with fear, appeared at the door of the hut, hands raised in surrender, while around him the big grinning Guardsmen lowered their rifles, as if both sides had played a nice little game of tennis, which their side had won. Next minute, he told himself, they would be giving the Huns cigarettes and showing them photographs of their kids and womenfolk back home. 'Christ,' he muttered to himself angrily, his face flushing as red as his hair, 'would the British never wake up to the real way to make war! Fight to win, show no mercy, and kill. That was the only way your enemies ever respected you.' He controlled his rage just in time. The men weren't ready yet for the kind of dog-eat-dog warfare he had learned in India and Palestine. But they'd learn in due course, they'd learn – he'd see to that. 'Sarnt-Major,' he snapped.

'Sir!' MacDonald routinely dug his bayonet in the snow and cleansed the burnished blade of the young man's blood.

'Get those prisoners back in the hut . . . and start the men up the road. The noise of firing could well have alerted some of their comrades back down there towards Narvik.'

'Sir!' Hurriedly MacDonald shouted some orders. The bewildered Germans were herded back into the shack and the first files of Guardsmen, spread out on alternate sides of the road leading into the mountains, began to move off.

MacDonald nodded his approval and then swung round on a waiting Red Rory. 'Permission to speak, sir?' he barked, using the standard formula of the Brigade of Guards when addressing an officer.

'Yes, Sarnt-Major?' Red Rory answered, taking his eyes off the heights. It was very grey up there, the sky leaden and threatening. Soon it would be snowing like hell; he knew the signs.

'The lads who copped a packet, sir. Guardsmen Maxwell and Chapman, what are we going to do with them – and the Jerry prisoners, too, sir?'

Red Rory looked at the two wounded Guardsmen. Maxwell lay on the ground groaning, his shattered knee packed in thick yellow wound bandages, already tinging pink with escaping blood. Chapman was in better shape. He was still upright, nursing his wounded shoulder, his face ashen with shock, puffing morosely at a Woodbine that one of his comrades had given him. The major frowned. 'Well, Sarnt-Major, they obviously can't go with the column. But Chapman doesn't look in too bad shape. I'll give him my Tommy-gun. He can guard the Huns and see that they look after Maxwell the best they can.' He raised his voice and lied glibly. 'Besides, the rest of the brigade should be here within the next twenty-four hours. Then they'll all receive proper care and medical attention.'

The huge NCO with the already greying hair frowned, as if not altogether convinced, but Red Rory did not give him a chance to object. MacDonald was an absolutely first-class NCO, he knew, but he tended to identify too much with the other ranks; his heart was too tender. 'All right Sarnt-Major, let's get to it. You take the head of the column. I'll bring up the rear. Usual march drill. Five minutes break for a cigarette after each hour. See the men observe strict water-bottle discipline. I don't want them without water up there and starting eating snow. It plays hell with the guts. All right, off you go.'

MacDonald seemed about to hesitate, but twenty-two years of iron discipline prevailed. He swung the major one of his immaculate salutes and then he was off, striding up the slope effortlessly on his long legs, easily out-distancing Guardsmen half his age.

Red Rory watched him go for a while. Then he nodded to the Huns. 'Take the wounded man inside,' he commanded in English.

The mountain troopers didn't speak English, but they understood the tone well enough. Gently they bent and picked up Maxwell. Carefully they carried him inside and placed the wounded Guardsman next to their own injured comrades.

The major turned to Chapman, pulling a packet of Gold Flake out of the pocket of his greatcoat, 'Here take these. There's twenty in there. Should keep you going until our chaps land.'

Chapman stiffened to attention with an effort and said thickly, face contorted with pain, 'Thank you, sir. I'll see old Bob's all right.'

'I'm sure you will,' Red Rory said, hearing his voice come from miles away, as his brain raced and he made his decision on what he would have to do next. 'You'd better get inside too. It's going to snow soon.'

'Permission to speak, sir?'

'Yes.'

'You said something about your Tommy-gun, sir, to the sarnt-major.'

'Did I?' Red Rory said coldly, his blue eyes full of that icy arrogance which had intimidated many a senior officer in the past.

Chapman swallowed hard. 'I'll be going in now, sir,' he said lamely.

'Yes, do that – and close the door. Keep the warmth in. Put the Huns at the far end of the shanty and keep your eye on them.'

'Sir.' Still the old brigade discipline held, in spite of the fact that Chapman knew he was being abandoned here in the back of nowhere. He clicked to attention, then without another word he turned, went into the hut and closed the heavy wooden door behind him.

Red Rory licked his lips which were suddenly very dry. He tried to calm his racing heart. It had to be done, and that was that, he told himself. A few Huns and two of his own chaps had to be sacrificed to save the lives of two hundred of their comrades and, above all, to ensure the success of the mission. Back on the North-West Frontier the Pathans had done the same thing with their wounded so they could not betray any secrets. In Palestine the Arabs had done it, too, slitting the skinny brown throats of their injured comrades where they lay in the sand. Why should the British be any different? If the Wogs could do it, surely they could?

Thus the tall arrogant major with the icy-blue dangerous eyes rationalized as he waited for the last file of Guardsmen to disappear over the rise beyond. He fumbled in his pocket, the same one in which he had found the gaspers for Chapman. This time he pulled out a small metal object, very ugly and very lethal, sizing up the stout stone walls as he did so and telling himself that they were exactly right. They'd hold in the blast, turning it onto those inside. He flashed a look up at the little chimney. There was no netting to keep out the mosquitos in summer. Just the job. The major waited no longer. He grunted softly as he pulled out the pin. The lever flew off with a slight metallic ping. Moving his dry lips as he did so, he counted off the seconds to death, '. . . *one . . . two . . . three* . . .' Hurriedly he lobbed it upwards. It sailed through the air, a deadly black whirling egg, and disappeared neatly down the chimney of the shack.

Next moment the murderer was pelting after the others as if the Devil himself were pursuing him.

*

'*Handgranate!*' one of the Germans screamed frantically, as the evil little metal object came tumbling out of the open fire, trailing sparks and embers after it.

'What?' Maxwell, lying next to the chimney, asked feebly.

'Christ, a fucking hand grenade!' Chapman yelled, too surprised to be frightened. '*What the f . . .*'

He never completed his question. There was an ear-shattering roar as a bright red-yellow ball of flame erupted in the centre of the shack. Chapman's ribcage collapsed and shards of shattered bone ripped his lungs apart. A gush of dark red blood jetted out of the hole in his face where his mouth had been, carrying the major's Gold Flake with it.

On the floor, the concussion picked up Guardsman Maxwell's body and hurled it against the wall. It slammed against the thick stone like a sack of wet cement. He died without ever knowing what had hit him, while around him the mountain troopers sprawled in bloody confusion, their stomachs burst open, spilling their steaming intestines onto the littered floor. Slowly now, as the last of them died horribly, the concussion ring circled the walls, pushing higher and higher, destroying everything in its path until finally it blew off the roof in one terminal *whoosh* of fury. A great smoke-ring of death like a Red Indian signal fire started to rise into the leaden sky . . .

A mile away, Sergeant-Major MacDonald heard the muffled boom down below. He turned, a little puzzled, letting the leading file of sweating, plodding Guardsmen move by him, backs bent under the weight of their loads. There was nothing to be seen save a cloud of smoke slowly rising behind the last ridge. 'Funny,' he said, pushing up his flat helmet and scratching his grizzled shaven head in bewilderment, 'very sodding funny.' Then he turned and hurried after the leading section, telling himself that they'd be hitting trouble soon, and the lads, as always, would need 'Old Daddy-MacDonald', as they called him behind his back.

And to the rear, Major Red Rory Ferguson slung the Tommy-gun he had promised Chapman – it was much too important a weapon for close-combat fighting to give to another rank – and told himself they were committed now. From this moment on, the parade-ground soldiering was over; now the real soldiering could commence . . .

## THREE

As the first scarlet flash of fire stabbed the white, Colonel Stuermer knew instinctively that the attack had begun. He stirred out of his snow hole with difficulty, although he realized the urgency of the moment, for his limbs were chilled and stiff after lying in the dead ground for nearly four hours now. 'Stand by, *Edelweiss!*' he yelled above the wind and the growing volume of enemy fire that was coming in from all sides. 'Greul, all right to the rear?'

With his usual fanatical bravery Greul raised the whole of his upper body and yelled back, his voice snatched by the wind that was carrying the snow and stinging tears from his eyes. 'All right to the rear, sir!' With fingers that felt as if they were clumsy sausages, he brought up his Schmeisser and whipped a control burst from left to right. All around him, his frozen troopers prepared for the attack.

Within seconds, visibility was down to a couple of metres. The defenders were blanketed in an almost impenetrable cocoon of swirling white icy flakes. Stuermer cursed. They would be lucky if they could survive an all-out Norwegian attack in this kind of shitting weather. The enemy would be able to get close enough without casualties to make full use of his superior numbers in one final mad dash for the *Edelweiss* positions; they were outnumbered at least four to one, they would be swamped. But when he spoke, his voice revealed none of his inner fears. 'Fire at will, comrades!' he cried above the howling wind. 'Don't worry about ammo for the time being. The main thing is to keep the hairy-assed bastards at a dist . . .'

A dark shape burst out of the gloom. It was one of the Wild Ones in a black hairy coat. Stuermer ducked instinctively, as a hunting rifle boomed and the air was filled with hundreds of flying pellets. They howled off the rocks murderously on all sides. Next moment he popped up again and fired without aiming. The Wild One fell back howling, the front of his bearded face torn away by the burst from the big colonel's machine pistol.

The Norwegians, soldiers and the civilians they called the Wild Ones, were everywhere in the whirling snow, trying to find the weak spots in the German defences, ready to throw in the full weight of their numbers once they had found the right place for the final attack.

Desperately, Stuermer and Major Greul, commanding front and rear of their impossible position, fought them off, taking crazy chances, as the enemy dominated the high ground, knowing that the snow was their only protection every time they raised themselves and exposed their bodies to the Norwegian fire.

The air was filled with the wild chatter of machine gun fire, the snap and crackle of small-arms, the crazy howls of the ricochets, the vicious stab and snap of muzzle flashes, as both sides fought and sought for the advantage.

Nature itself seemed to be taking sides. The wind howled in at a hundred kilometres an hour, slapping the defenders' faces in wild fury, whipping their crimson streaming cheeks like white tracer, blinding them momentarily, so that they blinked constantly, trying to clear their vision before they were swamped under the enemy's weight. Twice the Norwegians nearly broke the ring, taking heavy losses as they did so, being beaten off at the very last instant, leaving their corpses stacked up in front of the *Edelweiss* troopers like piles of abandoned logs. Then during a lull when a weary, down-hearted Stuermer told himself they would not survive the third charge that must come soon – this time the ring *had* to break under that impossible weight – there was a sudden sharp hiss that drowned even the roar of the snow-filled wind. Startled, Stuermer looked upwards. A crack. A kind of metallic ripping noise and there it was – blazing like a red angel of doom – a bright incandescent flare that coloured the falling snow a blood-red hue.

For a moment his mouth dropped open in wonder. What did it mean? Did it signify a co-ordinated Norwegian attack from front and rear? Or was it just the signal for the last attack?

'*Stormtroop Edelweiss, Stormtroop Edelweiss . . . do you hear me?*' A well-remembered voice came floating in to the hard-pressed men on the wind and Colonel Stuermer's heart gave a great leap of joy.

'Great Crap on the Christmas Tree!' a corporal gasped in awe and admiration next to him in the snow, '*it's him!*'

'It is indeed!' Stuermer yelled. Forgetting his own danger, he stood upright and cupped his hands around his mouth. 'Ox . . . we hear you . . . do you read me? . . . *WE HEAR YOU!*' He turned round to his perimeter defenders. 'Cease firing,' he commanded. 'Do you hear . . . cease firing . . . It's the Sergeant-Major!'

'Easy as falling off a log, sir,' Ox-Jo said proudly, neatly palming a flatman that Jap had just taken off one of the dead Norwegian soldiers and slipping it in his back-pocket, as he reported. He hoped it was aquavit. That stuff really packed a punch and that's exactly what he needed after this afternoon's work in the freezing cold. 'We caught them with their knickers down and their legs spread high in the air.'

'You really have an engaging way of making a military report, Ox,' Colonel Stuermer said, as the sound of the firing began to die away in the far distance and his men started to loot the bodies lying everywhere, the snow already blanketing them in a thin, charitable white mantle.

'I allus thought so, sir,' the big sergeant-major replied, for irony was always lost on him, or so it seemed. 'Anyway, sir, the good news is this,' he added, tapping the bulge of the flatman in his back pocket happily in greedy anticipation.

'What?'

'There's a shitting one-horse Norwegian hamlet, only a kilometre from here – to the south. These country yokels must live like pigs, but still it'd be a roof over the heads of the boys for the night and a nice log fire would be comforting, eh.' For some reason, he blushed.

Standing next to the noncom Jap knew why. He, too, had glimpsed the brawny Norwegian woman in the last hut, as they had raced to the rescue of their trapped comrades. He needed no crystal ball to know what the Bavarian barnshitter was thinking about at this very moment – and it didn't come in cans.

'Secure?' Stuermer asked.

'Absolutely, sir,' Ox-Jo replied with more conviction than he felt – but still there was the woman and he hadn't had a bit of nookie since Hamburg-Fullsbuttel, and that had been a five mark knee-trembler against the wall at the back of Hamburg *Hauptbahnhof*.

Stuermer considered for a moment, but only for a moment. The men were frozen through. They needed warmth and hot food; he had to take a chance that the Norwegians might resume their attacks. 'All right,' he cried above the howl of the wind, 'lead on you big rogue . . . Major Greul, bring up the rear . . . and for God's sake, let's get the hell out of here *now!*'

Five minutes later the survivors of *Stormtroop Edelweiss*'s first encounter with the new enemy had vanished into the whirling white gloom, leaving the snowfield to the dead and the hard red eyes of the Wild Ones for whom this barren wilderness was home . . .

Ox-Jo finished the last of the thick green peasoup from his canteen, belched in appreciation, raised one buttock to give a satisfied fart, then completed it all by wiping the dewdrop off the end of his red nose with his fingers. 'The inner pigdog is satisfied,' he announced, 'at least as far as food goes,' he added significantly, staring pointedly at the big Norwegian woman at the far end of the room, wreathed in the steam coming from the cooking pots.

Jap paused in his task of cleaning out the wax from his left ear with the point of his bayonet and sneered, 'Perfect Bavarian gentleman, aren't yer?'

'I was thinking,' Ox-Jo answered with no rancour, as if that were sufficient explanation.

Around them in the long, low-ceilinged timber hut the weary but fed mountain troopers were now wearily beginning to stretch out on the straw covered floor. Outside it was still snowing hard and the shutters rattled noisily in the keen wind.

'I suppose the mental strain activates your fart cannon?' Jap said sarcastically, flicking a particularly large piece of wax from the end of his bayonet into Ox-Jo's canteen.

'Sort of. But just you keep boring into your lughole. There's nothing to stop yer cutlass till it comes out of the other side of yer yellow turnip.' Suddenly he gasped, as if in awe, as the Norwegian woman turned round, the sweat glistening on her red face in the flickering yellow light of the storm lantern. 'Just feast yer glassy orbs on them lungs, willya?'

Jap's mouth dropped. Ox-Jo was right. The moon-faced mountain woman, with her blonde hair pulled tight into a bun at the back of her head, looked as if she had two sacks of potatoes tied together by a belt which then disappeared into the soft pillow of her billowing, massive stomach.

'I'd give my right arm, if she'd only bend down at this minute!' Ox-Jo groaned.

'If she did, she'd poke yer shitting eyes out with them tits,' Jap said unfeelingly. All the same he was impressed, very impressed.

'I wouldn't mind,' Ox-Jo answered in a faint little voice, as the woman stooped and took more water out of the enamel pail to wash the pots in which she had cooked the troopers' supper soup. 'Imagine cuddling yer head between them lungs, Jap,' he breathed, 'my God, you wouldn't be able to hear a thing for days afterwards!'

Jap sniffed. 'I might have a go at her myself afterwards,' he declared confidently, 'she's about my collar size.'

'*You?*' Ox-Jo cried incredulously, taking his entranced gaze off the woman for a while, the first loud snores cutting the thick fug of the tight room and indicating that the *Edelweiss* men were bedding down for the night now.

'Yer, me,' Jap answered, finishing his self-imposed task and wiping the end of his bayonet on the sleeve of Ox-Jo's jacket, which lay on the wooden bench between them.

'Piss off!' Ox-Jo snorted. 'That's a real female woman up there. She wants, no *demands*, a real piece of Nordic sausage as her right. She knows what the Führer wants for us Aryans. Not a little tiny bit of dried Asiatic tripe like what you've got dangling between yer inferior legs. Why, it would be almost like . . .' he fumbled for words, so great was his apparent indignation . . . 'an act of racial impurity!'

Jap was unmoved. 'Watch it,' he warned, 'don't get yourself excited or you'll be having one of your migraine attacks agen. You know how you are at this time of the month. Why don't you just get yer head down with a cup of weak herbal tea and yer Goethe poems?'

'I'll stuff Goethe and his poems up yer little yellow fart-cannon in half a mo – *sideways!*' Ox-Jo threatened.

Jap answered calmly. 'Let's do it like this,' he said in tones of sweet reason itself. 'It's as clear as the hooter at the end of your ugly face that we can't both get inside those pearly gates together, isn't it?' He flashed a quick look at the woman, who was bent over the stove again, displaying an enormous rump, 'though, I don't know,' he added. 'Well, I'll score first and then when she's recovered from me, I'll hand her over to you. I know that she won't ever again want another man after she's had me,' he ended, his wizened yellow face full of self-confident pride, 'but I'll put in a good word for you. I'll tell her you're my brother or something . . . Now how does that sound, Ox?'

'*How does* . . .' Ox-Jo caught himself exploding just in time; he didn't want to wake the men who were already sleeping, '. . . does that sound? It sounds like shit. It's perverted! It's a crime against nature! It's not decent . . . it's . . . Besides I'm senior in rank to you,' he ended lamely.

And there the discussion ended for the time being and the two comrades sat at the trestle table, faces slumped into their hands, watching every move the Norwegian woman made, while outside the wind howled and the sentries' boots crunched noisily on the deep snow as they marched their beat.

Stuermer and Major Greul were also not yet asleep although both officers were exhausted after the day's events; and it was not the howl of the wind that kept them awake. Crouched in the little room, which apparently held fodder for the upland cattle in summer, lit by the flickering light of a candle placed in a saucer, both men worried about their predicament and their plans for the morrow.

'I suggest we break for the coastal plain tomorrow, sir,' Greul said, his voice unusually low. Perhaps he was awed, too, by the same sense of loneliness, remoteness, that afflicted Stuermer. 'I hate to run from that Norwegian rabble out there somewhere, but it would allow us to contact General Dietl and assure him that we are covering his rear against any enemy movement.'

Stuermer, huddled up in his sleeping bag for warmth, nodded. 'I agree, Greul. But I don't think we should make it too obvious that we are withdrawing. It might well make the enemy overconfident and we could have a running fight on our hands.'

Greul indicated he agreed. 'What do you suggest, sir?'

'The main body to slip out at dawn, leaving a rearguard

to cover until they, in their turn, move out. As soon as it's light the enemy who, we can assume, is watching this place, will believe that we're sending out a minor patrol and leave them in peace. We can then rendezvous at an agreed map reference and make a speedy march to the littoral.'

'I volunteer to command the rearguard, sir,' Greul snapped, the Prussian soldier to the very end, even in this God-forsaken place.

In spite of his weariness, Stuermer grinned. 'No, my dear Greul, you are far too valuable to be wasted on the rearguard. You'll take the point.'

Greul concealed his disappointment, perhaps flattered by Stuermer's comment. 'Well, who will take charge of the ones who stay behind, sir?'

'Me,' Stuermer said simply and smiled. 'After all, a captain has to go down with his sinking ship, you know, though,' he added hastily, 'I have no intention whatsoever of letting that particular eventuality take place. Now, Greul, let's dowse the candle and get some sleep. Remember you'll have to be up well before dawn and get the men started. Good night.'

Greul obediently leaned out of his bag and blew out the candle. 'Good night, sir,' he said. He turned over on his side and went to sleep immediately.

Stuermer, lying on his back, hands folded under his head, trying to penetrate the gloom above his head, grinned. Greul was so damn well organized. He was the perfect soldier. He could make himself go to sleep on command.

Then he forgot Greul, gently snoring at his side. Suddenly he realized he was happy in this remote place, in spite of the danger. He was back in his beloved mountains, away from the gaudy brutality of the Third Reich to which he had been forced to belong, although he hated its jackbooted cruelty and lethal pomposity, because he was a German first and a professional mountaineer and climber second. He was once again in the high peaks, with its cleaner air and simple black-and-white values, where a man could be a man and Nature would let you survive or die unfeelingly, leaving it to you to make the attempt – or not. Whatever the morrow might bring, he knew that he could face it confidently, almost happily. He sighed, turned on his side and fell asleep instantly.

Now the little hamlet slept, no sound disturbing their slumbers save the soft crunch of the sentries' boots on the falling snow, the snores of the exhausted men, the slap of angry cards on the wooden table, as Jap and Ox-Jo gambled on who would have the first chance at the massive favours of the woman sitting quietly by the fire waiting for their decision, and the harsh breathing of the Wild Ones, muffled up in their wolfskin furs, watching and waiting . . .

# FOUR

'Grab her!' Larsen growled urgently, as the door opened and a yellow knife of light slid into the whirling snow. 'Quick!'

Captain Helge of the Telemark Regiment, crouched next to him in the flying snow at the edge of the hamlet, frowned. 'What do you want the woman for, Larsen?' he asked the burly bearded hunter, whose smell was so animal and rancid that he could hardly bear being within ten metres of him.

'She's been with the Fritzes,' Larsen snarled, 'and she can give us info. That's why, soldier-boy.'

'I wish you wouldn't call me that, Larsen,' Helge snapped. 'After all, I *am* a regular officer in the Royal Norwegian Army.'

Larsen grunted an obscenity and watched as his men stole towards the woman squatting in the triangle of light, obviously relieving herself. They moved silently and swiftly like the half-wild animals they were, brutalized and coarsened by the years they had spent living alone in these high peaks trapping the animals, whose pelts they sold in the coastal towns for the pathetic handful of *kronen* that fat, greasy flatland Jews gave them.

While the army captain still peered helplessly into the whirling gloom, unable to make out anything but the fat woman squatting urinating noisily in the patch of yellow light cast on the snow, Larsen, at his side, watched his men steal in between the patrolling Fritz sentries and begin to work their way along the length of the hut towards the unsuspecting bitch, whose heat had been well dampened now by the Fritzes, he had no doubt. If it hadn't, he told himself grimly, his evil bearded face breaking suddenly into a wolfish smile of anticipation, it soon would be once *he* got his paws on her.

The woman began to rise, adjusting her thick clothes, wiping herself, preparing to enter the comforting thick fug of the hut. That wasn't to be. Abruptly a dark shadow detached itself from the side of the building. He could see just how the woman stiffened. Perhaps she was opening her mouth to scream, for abruptly the man in the shadows shot his fist out hard. She dropped as if pole-axed. The man bent down and effortlessly threw her great bulk over his shoulder. Next instant he had disappeared back into the shadows from whence he had come.

Noiselessly Larsen rose from the snow. 'Come,' he ordered.

'But why . . . what happened?' Captain Helge stuttered, confused, telling himself again that he had been a fool not to surrender on the coast while he had had a chance. God, what in heaven's name did he want with these barbarians?

'We've got her,' Larsen said scornfully, looking down in contempt at the captain. 'The woman . . . She's ours . . .'

'*Traitor!*' Larsen cried and hit the woman across the face. She reeled back, blood spurting from her nose. Larsen caught her just before she fell into the log fire.

Helge gulped hard.

'*German whore!*' Larsen ripped down the front of her peasant blouse, and her enormous breasts tumbled out and fell to her waist like two monstrous puddings. The woman started to sob, shoulders heaving, tears coursing down her bloodstained face.

'I really must protest, Larsen!' Helge commenced.

'Shut your pansy trap!' Larsen cut him off brutally, not taking his evil black eyes off the woman. 'Well, are you going to tell me what the Fritzes are up to or not, wench?' He hit her again and she howled as fresh blood spurted from her nostrils, began to trickle down her chin, mixed with green thick mucus.

The woman was used to beatings. Ever since the farmer had chosen her from the orphanage down on the coast to work for him and duly, at the age of fourteen when she had come of age, had taken her virginity, with his plump wife's consent, men had beaten her and then screwed her afterwards. It was a fact of life and although she cried and moaned as now, she was not really badly hurt; she was tough. In the mountains with so few women and men who were mostly illiterate farmers or Wild Ones, as these were, a woman had to be strong. The Fritzes hadn't been bad sorts as men went. The little one who had poked her first had even given her money, which at present nestled at the top of her thick woollen stocking, held up by a black elastic garter, where the likes of Larsen wouldn't find it. She wiped the muck away from her nose and stopped sobbing. 'What do you want to know, sir?' she said thickly, tasting the salt blood that came from her split lip.

'Don't call me *sir*, you impudent cunt!' Larsen slapped her again.

Captain Helge bit his bottom lip. Larsen, the self-appointed leader of the Wild Ones, obviously enjoyed hitting people. Why, in God's name, hadn't he surrendered to the Fritzes while there had still been time?

'Sorry,' the woman said thickly, supporting herself against the crude log table, which together with the sleeping benches, heavy with stinking furs, provided the hut's sole furniture. 'I . . .' She saw the look in Larsen's eyes and said hastily, 'I'll tell you anything I know.'

'Good,' Larsen grunted, a little appeased, 'but I warn you, wench, one lie and I'll stick that log up yer cunt. Then even the Fritzes won't want yer.' Routinely, he grabbed one of her great dugs and pulled her to him, taking pleasure in the grimace of pain that contorted her moonlike peasant face. 'How many of them are there left?'

She told him with a gasp.

He dug the long, sharp-pointed nail of his little finger into her nipple. The hunters always left the little nails long; it was a ritual vanity with them. He pressed hard and she screamed, as the nipple started to bleed. 'You're sure you're telling me the truth?' he urged, exerting more and more pressure until she thought the swine would rip it right off.

'*Tak, tak . . .*' she gasped fervently. 'I swear it – *in God's name!*'

He pulled the nail out. Blood was trickling down that monstrous breast now and dripping onto the vast yellow mound of her swollen stomach. 'Good, now what do they intend to do?'

She looked at Larsen's savage face in confusion. 'Do . . . now?' she stuttered. Didn't her torturer realize that men had never told her anything in all her life; they just took her, did with her what they liked, and left her.

'Sow,' Larsen cursed. 'One minute more and I'll cut off your tits and burn them in front of your eyes, then I'll make you eat the ashes. Now speak!'

'All I know is that . . .' But she never finished. There was the sudden hiss of skis outside. In a flash Larsen had unslung his hunting rifle and Captain Helge had pulled out his pistol, every man in the room tense and expectant, the girl forgotten. From outside there came a muffled challenge, followed by an excited explanation. A moment later the door was flung open, flooding the room with icy night air. A tall man stood there, clad in the uniform of the Royal Norwegian Army. He saw the captain and clicked to attention awkwardly. 'Sir,' he said, 'an important message from General Ruge[1].'

Larsen's face twisted into a sneer and he said, 'For God's sake, stop all this play-acting and toy-soldiering. This isn't the changing of the guard outside the Royal Palace, you know.' He reached out a big dirty paw to take the message but Helge beat him to it.

[1] Commander-in-Chief of the Norwegian Army.

Hastily, he unfolded the buff-coloured form and read the message out aloud, while on the floor the girl slumped in her bloodstained rags sobbed softly. 'The English have landed north of Narvik. A reinforced company marching to join up with you. Advise immediate contact. English going to land in strength of one brigade Narvik next twenty-four hours. Ruge.'

Helge looked up in triumph, as if the message vindicated his presence there. The army, his face said, hadn't let the civilians down after all. 'Well, Larsen,' he said, new energy in his voice, 'what do you say to that?'

Larsen attempted his old sneer, but unsuccessfully. He knew, too, that once troops were present in strength, his importance would diminish. All those high-class officers with their posh accents and fancy city ways would have no time for the likes of him and his Wild Ones. 'What we gonna do then?' he asked grudgingly.

'This. For the time being we'll forget the Germans back there in the hamlet. There'll be time and enough for them later and they are so few that they can present no danger to a whole brigade of English soldiers. That's three thousand men, you know,' he added, airing his knowledge to a now sulky Larsen, who realized how swiftly power was slipping through his fingers. 'Now that English company the general mentioned, that will be the brigade's reconnaissance force, I should imagine. They'll be probing for the weak spot in Narvik's defences, sort of a pin . . .'

'Don't shit around, soldier-boy!' Larsen interrupted crudely. 'Get on with it. What are we supposed to do, me and my boys?'

'You'll join with my platoon and link up with the English,' Helge said with regained authority. 'You know this high plateau like the back of your – exceedingly dirty,' he beamed at Larsen maliciously, '*paw!* You will be of some use to us scouts so that we soldiers can get on with the fighting. Then, when we've given the Germans a sound thrashing and turfed them out of Narvik, you and your fellows can go back to your hunting.'

Larsen opened his mouth to say something, but the captain gave him no time. His position restored now, he turned to the messenger, 'Take this signal for General Ruge, Corporal.' Hurriedly he dictated his message to the soldier. 'Sergeant,' he snapped to his platoon NCO, 'get the men fallen in in ten minutes. Full marching order, complete with skis. We'll need them. It's snowing hard.'

The NCO followed the messenger out to execute the order. Helge waited till the door closed behind them, cutting off the howl of the wind before swinging on Larsen and saying, 'Well, come on, man, don't just stand there . . . Get your fellows cracking as well. Time is of the essence!'

Larsen seemed about to object, but changed his mind. He aimed a vicious kick at the girl sobbing on the floor, taking his rage out on her. She yelped with pain, but didn't raise her bloody, bruised head so that her tormentor could see the look in her eyes. 'All right, Ohlsen . . . Svenson,' he growled, 'don't hang around with your thumbs up yer lazy arses! Round up the men . . . Let's get out of here.'

Helge grinned. He had well and truly taken the wind out of Larsen's sails. The brute had had his moment of power. Now he was just as simple and very unpleasant peasant once again. And on the floor the girl continued to sob, as if heartbroken, playing for time, waiting till the beasts had gone. The realization was growing in her poor simple mind that she had the power to pay these men back for their Norwegian cruelty, pay them all back for the way they had treated her ever since the farmer had thrown her in the hay, ripped off her pants and raped her in dogged panting silence. Yes, they'd pay . . .

# FIVE

Visibility was zero.

As the Scots Guards toiled up the steep ascent, they were blanketed from time to time by the whirling, impenetrable, icy cocoon of vicious white. Doubled up against the wind which howled like a banshee, and whipped the snow against their crimson, streaming faces, threatening to blow them off the mountain more than once, the big soldiers floundered on, each man preoccupied by his own misery.

Sergeant-Major MacDonald, laden with two extra rifles taken from Guardsmen who were weakening, told himself that Major Ferguson was a tower of strength. He had all the arrogance and imperturbability of the old pre-war Guards officer but, all the same, he also had the kind of endurance and stamina not common to the gents he had known in the old days. Like MacDonald, he, too, was carrying two rifles in addition to the Tommy-gun, which somehow he had retained, plunging up and down the long column cajoling, threatening, joking with the men, keeping them going by sheer willpower. Once one of the older men, Williamson from Perth, had virtually collapsed, but Ferguson had kept him going. 'Sorry to be such a bluidy nuisance, sir,' Williamson had gasped, eyes liquid with pain and fatigue, face caked with snow, 'but ye ken, mà legs they're no what they were.'

'It's all right, Williamson,' the major had reassured him, even forcing a smile and, placing his arm under the big Scot, he had managed to keep him going until he had found his strength again.

Yes, MacDonald had to admit to himself that, although he had his doubts about Major Ferguson, if anyone was capable of getting the company through this murderous cruel terrain, it would be the big red-haired Laird.

Another terrible hour passed. Now the Guardsmen were slogging up a treacherous slope, made doubly difficult by the new snow, the wind screeching furiously all-out, threatening to pluck them off their feet, every fresh step sheer torture, the snow sticking to their boots in huge clumps so that the effort of lifting made their legs burn with agonizing pain. Time and time again, men slipped, the howl of that awesome wind muffling their curses and cries. MacDonald stumbled and fell with them, physically fighting off the almost overwhelming temptation to just lie there in the soft seductive embrace of the snow and let happen what may. Each time he fought off the temptation, summoning up the last of his strength, hardly knowing where it came from, and continued that brutal, lung-rasping, nightmarish climb. On and on, as if it would never end . . .

Two hours after daylight, the force of the snow blizzard began to lessen. The wind dropped and the big soldiers found they could start to breathe more easily. No longer did the gale snatch the very breath from their mouths. Finally at about ten o'clock the snow stopped altogether, and a faint yellow sun edged its way shyly over the peaks, illuminating the snowfield in a gleaming white crystalline hue. Abruptly they had to narrow their eyes to slits against the glare.

Ferguson nodded his snow-covered head to MacDonald and the big NCO breathed an inward sigh of relief. It was the signal for a break, and the lads certainly needed one after what they had been through this night.

He raised his voice and pointed to a line of pines, sparkling in the new snow. 'All right, you shower, get fell out – over there!' He turned to Major Ferguson, as the men started to trudge towards the trees, their faces lighting up at the prospect of a rest after the hard slog. 'Permission to make a brew-up, sir?' he asked formally.

'Permission granted,' Ferguson answered, 'and let them

have some kind of meal. They can heat up the M and V tins, if they like, and eat two of the hardtack biscuits.'

'Thank you, sir.' In spite of his weariness, MacDonald threw the officer a tremendous salute and went off to carry out his orders.

Red Rory didn't follow. He knew MacDonald would do everything perfectly well; he couldn't have wished for a better NCO in charge. Instead he fumbled for his glasses with fingers that felt like clumsy sausages and focused on the sparkling slopes and peaks ahead of them. He did so deliberately, taking his time, although he could already hear the men lighting their fires and pumping the little Tommy-cookers to make the flame burn bright and hot. Sweeping the horizon from left to right systematically, pausing at every shadow and studying it carefully for any sign of movement or anything suspicious, he looked for danger. But there was none. The high plateau was empty. He nodded his approval, telling himself in the fashion of lonely men who speak to themselves, 'All's well. We could be the last men on earth.'

'Sir.'

He turned round a little startled.

It was MacDonald again. 'Your batman's brewing up, sir. The char'll be ready in a brace of shakes, and he's heating a tin of M and V for you as well, sir.' He grinned, 'And even Hawkins can't burn M and V, sir,' he added.

Ferguson returned the grin for a flash. Hawkins, his batman, was reputed to be able to burn hot water, he was such a bad cook. 'Thank you, Sarnt-Major. I'm looking forward to the tea. I'll see to the men in a moment and I think, although we're not officially in action, we could break out the rum this once and give each man a tot. What think you?'

'Ay, that's the stuff, sir!' MacDonald agreed, heartily. 'You know the Jocks, they'd go to hell and back for a dram.'

'Well, I hope they don't have to go that far, but I know

what you mean. Before we go over and have a look at the chaps, let me put you in the big picture.'

MacDonald's smile vanished immediately. He was all soldier now, respectful and attentive.

'Now this is the drill. As you know, we've outflanked the Hun positions in Narvik. If my compass is giving me a correct reading,' he tapped the instrument strapped to his wrist by a leather band, 'and compasses tend to go off a bit so close to magnetic north, then we should be somewhere to the rear of Narvik, almost due south of the place. Between it and the port itself is the railway line which leads to Sweden. The Huns import – indirectly – most of the Swedish ore by this route and then send it on to Germany itself. Now the holding of that railway line is much more important to them than Narvik itself. What can they do with the port if the Royal Navy blocks its exit? Understand?'

'Yessir,' MacDonald answered dutifully, already aware of what the major's plan would be. However, in the Brigade of Guards NCOs, even senior ones, were not encouraged to have thoughts on tactics or strategy; that was a province reserved solely for 'officers and gentlemen'.

'So it is my intention to do this.' Major Ferguson flashed the giant sergeant-major one of his rare wintry smiles. 'Quite contrary to what I told the general, incidentally, but then, between you and me, Sarnt-Major, the general is something of an old woman. Break the line somewhere down there. Pick an important junction or something of that kind and draw the Huns to me. They'll rise to the fly just like a fat salmon and come for us. If we make our defence serious enough, we'll pull the whole shower of them out of Narvik and then the general can really march his precious brigade into Narvik with his men at the slope. Now what do you say to that, Sarnt-Major?'

'They'll hit us hard, sir,' MacDonald said slowly, 'the Jerry, I mean.' He remembered the Imperial Guard Reserve Division back in September '18. They had been tall skinny blond boys and the officers had told them they were being chained to their machine guns to make them fight while the rest of the German Army had begun their final retreat. But that hadn't been true; he knew it and all the rest of the Jocks had known it. 'Old Jerry', as they'd called him, not without affection in those days, had been a bloody good fighter right to the bitter end. 'They'll come at us with all they've got,' he emphasized.

Ferguson frowned, as if he wished he hadn't taken the giant NCO into his confidence, then shrugged. 'We're the Scots Guards, aren't we?' he said, as if that were explanation enough.

MacDonald knew his place. 'Yessir,' he rapped dutifully. 'Would you be so kind as to look at the men now, sir?'

Ferguson nodded. He would be 'so kind'.

'Did you know that the Tommies invented mountain climbing?' Colonel Stuermer said, deliberately trying to annoy Greul, as the two of them spooned their thick pea soup from their canteens, enjoying the thin but warming rays of the sun which had appeared after the storm.

Greul frowned and bit hard on the black bread. 'The English are an effete and decadent nation,' he grunted. 'The nineteenth century wore them out. The twentieth belongs to the Reich. It is the German century.'

'The English rich started to climb because they were sick of the commercialism of city life. They wanted a new challenge after the challenge of making a fortune in cotton, coal and the like,' Stuermer persisted.

Greul swallowed the last of his bread ration, one slice per man per day, and tried not to notice the fact that Sergeant-Major Meier was drinking from what was obviously a flat bottle of spirits. Sometimes he wished that Colonel Stuermer would be harder on the men; he treated them almost as equals, though on reflection, he told himself, that equality of German man with German

man was what the Führer was trying to encourage. 'I don't admire them. I don't trust them. I don't fear them, Colonel,' he said dogmatically. 'The English have had their day. We shall win this war.'

Stuermer shrugged. 'Perhaps you're right, Greul,' he said, knowing that even in this remote corner of the earth one should not express that kind of thought so openly. There would already be a couple of Gestapo men attached to Dietl's headquarters in Narvik; there always were. It had been the same in Czechoslovakia, Austria and Poland; it would be the same in Norway, he had no doubt of that.

'The English didn't want this war,' Greul said. 'They were talked into it by the Jewish media and that Jew Roosevelt in Washington. They have no heart for the fight. It is my opinion that they will make a token resistance and then submit a plea for peace to the Führer. It is the only way that they are going to save their Empire. If they don't . . .' He stopped short.

Colonel Stuermer was no longer listening. Instead his gaze was fixed on the glittering crystalline snowfield, as was that of the men, who had even forgotten to eat, their curiosity was so great.

'What's the matter, sir?'

Then he saw it too. A dark shape was making its way across that brilliant white field, staggering from side to side, as if drunk, occasionally falling, crawling sometimes, but in the end uprighting itself and continuing its tortuous progress towards them. Hastily, he and Stuermer dropped their canteens and, pulling out their glasses, focused on the dark shape.

'In three devils' name,' Stuermer gasped, as two huge breasts barely covered by the tattered blouse came into view. 'It's a woman!'

'Yes, the one from the hamlet who disappeared last night,' Greul confirmed, not able even in this situation to repress his look of disapproval. Greul didn't like women, not because he was homosexual, but because they took a man's mind off the real purpose of life: to climb mountains, win wars, and gain ever more honour for Germany and the Führer.

Stuermer allowed his glasses to drop to his chest. 'Sergeant-Major Meier,' he called to where the men crouched, resting, 'get over to that female and see what's wrong!'

'Sir,' Ox-Jo bellowed back.

Jap winked and nudged him slyly. 'Didn't I tell yer, Ox, when I've had 'em, they stay had. She's probably been following us all day to get some more of the same.'

But Ox-Jo wasn't listening. 'You and you . . .' he rapped to the two nearest troopers, 'get over to her . . . and keep yer dirty paws off her lungs, do you understand. Or both of yer'll be lacking a set of teeth right quick!'

The woman was almost hysterical. She threw her arms around a suddenly embarrassed Jap, almost submerging his head in those huge breasts, sobbing and jabbering in her own language, the tears streaming down her bruised, battered face, clutching Jap to her, as if she would never let go of him again.

Stuermer gently drew his own blanket over her frozen shoulders and said to Ox-Jo, who was staring in amazement at the little scene, 'Break out that illegal flatman of yours, Ox, and give the poor wretch a drink. She's frozen and about all-in.'

Somehow or other they managed to separate her from Jap and force a hefty slug of the potent white spirit down her throat, which set her off coughing alarmingly but stopped her keening. Stuermer waited a minute and then gave her his handkerchief, indicating that she should clean up her face. It was obvious that she had been badly beaten up. There was caked blood at her nostrils, her upper lip was split and the skin beneath her right eye was puffy and swollen and green.

'What happened?' he asked gently.

Her reply was a burst of excited Norwegian.

He shook his head to indicate he didn't understand

her. She clutched his arm urgently and again poured out a torrent of words in her own harsh, seemingly monotonous tongue. Suddenly she had an idea. She knelt down and indicated that they should kneel too. Curiously, the men did so, while she waited impatiently. Then she hastily poked her finger in the fresh snow, one of her great dugs falling from beneath the blanket in her rush, and scribbled, 'NA' in it. 'Narvik,' she said, drawing out the syllables like people do when they speak to someone they think very stupid.

'Narvik,' Stuermer repeated and nodded his understanding.

She smiled and then drew a ship in the snow near the port, the kind of ship a six-year-old draws, writing an 'E' above it and making *boom-boom* noises, turning her head to them constantly to see if they had understood.

'English ships,' Greul said hurriedly and she nodded eagerly, as if she had understood the German.

The Norwegian woman went to work, sketching in an arrow coming from the ship to Narvik and then following that by another arrow coming from the rear, this time marked 'N' and 'E'. Finally she tucked away her breast like a man putting a wallet in his inside pocket and waited, smiling at them encouragingly, willing them to understand, saying '*Norge* . . .*Norge*' over and over again.

For a while they puzzled over the crude sketch, wondering what the combination of 'N' and 'E' coming obviously to their own rear could mean.

'*Norge*,' the girl said yet once again. '*Norge*.'

'*Norwegian*,' Jap said suddenly, snapping his fingers. 'That's what *Norge* means, I think.'

The girl nodded eagerly, a great smile on her pathetic, moon-shaped face and Jap stepped back hastily in case she should take it into her stupid head to embrace him once again. God, last time she'd nearly smothered him!

'That's it,' Stuermer said. 'The Tommies have landed to our rear and have linked up with the Norwegians, probably with the same lot that ambushed us. Now they're heading for . . .'

He stopped short. The girl had seemingly remembered something else, for she bent low again and with a forefinger drew what appeared to be a locomotive in the snow behind 'NA', making the *chug-chugging* sounds that infants do when they pretend to be an engine. 'So that's it,' Stuermer understood immediately. 'This force inland is to head for the railway line and you know what that means, Greul?'

Greul nodded grimly, 'I do, sir. Narvik has no value without the railway. That Swedish ore is vital to the Reich's war industries. General Dietl will be forced to defend it.'

'And leave Narvik wide open for the Tommies,' Stuermer snapped.

'Exactly.'

Stuermer wasted no further time. Five minutes later the men of *Edelweiss* were on their way westwards, leaving the girl still clad in the colonel's blanket, clutching all the rest of the *krone* the troopers possessed, staring after them in bewilderment, too dazed even to realize that she was holding more money in her work-hardened red hand than she had ever seen before . . .

# SIX

The Norwegians were amateurs. Stuermer, crouched with the rest of his men in the ambush, could see that. They bunched together, and their scouts, clad in black and perfect targets against the white, were too close to the main body. But, he told himself, it was all to the good. There were at least three hundred of them and they outnumbered his own small force two to one. 'Pass the word,' he whispered to Ox-Jo next to him, 'no one to fire without permission. Move out immediately when I give the order. Down the cliff-face. I doubt if they'll be able to follow us down there.'

Ox-Jo did as he was commanded, while Stuermer tensed and waited for the battle to commence. He knew he had no hope of defeating the Norwegians; he hadn't the heavy weapons he would need for that. But he did believe he could delay them long enough to reach the railway line somewhere in the coastal plain below before they were able to link up with the Tommies. This one would be hit and run.

Squatting next to him, Ox-Jo let the first of the men in the dark furs move into the round metal circle of his sight. He hadn't understood very much of what the Norwegian woman had told them before they had left, but it had been enough to make him hate these Wild Ones; they were the ones who had tortured her. Now he would pay the debt back. Grimly he followed the man with his sight, while he waited for the CO's command, tucking the stock well into the hollow formed by his chin and big shoulder.

Stuermer waited. They were walking into the trap as if they were hunters innocently plodding after game, not realizing that this particular game hit back. They were some three hundred metres away now. At that range even the worst shot among the *Edelweiss* troopers could not miss. He caught his breath. It was the moment he always hated: the moment of decision when he had to give the command that would result in the death of a fellow human being. It was never easy and he doubted if it ever would be, even if the war went on for a century. He counted off the seconds. One . . . two . . . three . . . Then he raised himself slightly and cried, '*Fire!*'

Ox-Jo hesitated for only a fraction of a second then he gently squeezed the trigger. The rifle slapped against his shoulder – hard. Down below Larsen screamed shrilly and started to fall, his startled gaze fixed on the gory mess of what had once been his genitals; for Ox-Jo had aimed deliberately at the spot below his guts. Next instant he fell face forwards into the snow and his long bubbling screams were cut off.

But there were others. The completely surprised Norwegians went down on all sides. Suddenly galvanized into frenetic activity, they were bowled over by the weight of the fire pouring into them, slapped against the boulders by the impact of the slugs, doubling crazily for cover, as the volley ripped the leading groups apart.

Scarlet flame stabbed the grey of the day everywhere. Behind the boulders, the survivors of that first unexpected volley began to return the German fire awkwardly and raggedly. Bullets whined off the rocks or erupted in white spurts of snow ahead of Stuermer. A heavy machine gun opened up ponderously, angrily, like an irritated, ancient woodpecker. The line of bullets ran the length of the Stormtroop's positions. The Norwegians were reacting. They were beginning to recover from the shock of the sudden attack, though the twenty-odd shapes sprawled out awkwardly in the snow would never recover now. They were dead.

'Major Greul!' Stuermer yelled above the burr of the machine gun and the howl of the ricochets.

'Sir!'

'We're breaking off the action now! I think we've put

a right scare into them. Start taking the main party down the cliff-face. I'll cover the rear.'

'But, sir . . .'

'Get on with it!' Stuermer interrupted brutally. He had no time for Greul's would-be heroics. '*GO!*'

'*Mir nach!*' Greul yelled and the men assigned to his command broke off firing, squirming out of their positions, and then when they felt they were in dead ground, ran heavily through the snow towards the edge of the cliff where Greul was already waiting to supervise the difficult descent.

Somehow the Norwegians sensed that something was happening, for a hoarse yell went up from below, whether in rage or in encouragement, Stuermer did not know nor care. Suddenly the Norwegian soldiers and the Wild Ones rose to their feet as one and swept forward in a rough-and-ready skirmish line, firing from the hip as they ran, yelling wildly.

'Standfast, men!' Stuermer cried, rising to his feet and exposing himself to the wild hail of new fire. He had to keep the men in position. A retreat at this particular stage, with half the men of the Stormtroop not even having commenced the descent, would be disastrous – sheer murder. Ignoring the tracer cutting the air viciously all around him, he fired carefully controlled bursts of mp fire to left and right, trying to knock the steam out of the surprise attack before they were overwhelmed.

'Come on, yer fucking heroes,' Ox-Jo yelled suddenly springing to his feet, inspired by the CO's example, 'do you want to live for ever? Let's show the fish-eating fuckers what real German soldiers are!' He sprang to his feet and started pumping bullet after bullet at their attackers.

The old trick worked. Carried away by the crazy bloodlust of combat, the rest of the *Edelweiss* troopers sprang out of their hiding places, guns blazing, spraying the running Norwegians with lead. They went down everywhere and, almost immediately, the steam went out of their attack. Men went reeling to the snow on all sides, some screaming piteously with the sudden agony of their wounds, others simply taking cover. Stuermer fired a full burst and then told himself, now was the time to pull out the rearguard; that mad volley would keep the Norwegians at bay for a while. 'Cease fire . . . cease fire!' he bellowed, fitting a new magazine to his Schmeisser. 'Ox, start pulling them back to the rock face . . . I'll cover you, firing a burst at regular intervals to make them think we're still up here . . . All right, off you go – *now!*'

'You're quite right, sir,' Sergeant MacDonald agreed, 'that was firing all right . . . and it was no rifle range stuff either,' he added, still straining his ears, 'that was the real thing.' Funny, he told himself, it was the first shots he had heard fired in anger since 1918. Now, he wondered, how would he act when he came under real fire again twenty-two years later and with a son older than he had been then in the trenches? He dismissed the thought as quickly as it had come. He was an NCO in the Brigade of Guards, wasn't he? There was only one way that a Guardsman should behave. Bravely.

The Laird pushed back his helmet impatiently and scratched his bright red thatch. 'It can only be the Huns and the Norwegians, Sarnt-Major,' he said almost angrily. 'They've clashed somewhere up there. Hm. It's obvious, too, that they're not far from that damned railway line.' He flung a glance at the map attached to his waist in the khaki-covered case. 'I make it another seven miles to the nearest section of railway.'

'Nearly two hours' march, sir,' MacDonald made the calculation for him dutifully, as was expected of a good senior noncom.

'Yes, that's the damned rub. They could be there and be dug in before we make it, then we're in for a real fight and I don't think the chaps are up to an all-out attack after the last twenty-four hours.'

'No, sir,' MacDonald agreed, looking at his weary Guardsmen, resting their packs against the trees trying to ease the weight for a few moments. 'They've taken a bit of a bashing. But they'll be all right after some hot food and a bit of a rest.'

Major Ferguson turned on him with unexpected anger. 'There'll be no hot food and no rest, Sarnt-Major!' he barked harshly. 'This is *not* Aldershot and we are *not* on manoeuvres, do you understand that?'

'Yessir,' MacDonald answered, taken aback by the sudden venom.

'Good, now order the men to dump their big packs, their overcoats. We'll move on just in battle order. It'll make their load less and they'll move quicker that way.'

'But, sir, in this cold, without their greatcoats . . .' His voice faltered. The officer wasn't listening. Already he had begun to fumble with the brass buckles of his own pack. MacDonald turned and crossed to the waiting men to convey the major's orders.

Five minutes later they were off again, trying to keep up with Major Ferguson who was setting a cracking pace, leaving behind them their greatcoats and packs, containing all the bits and pieces that linked them with Scotland, lying in the snow like dead bodies . . .

Like flies crawling along the gleaming silver envelope of some gigantic Zeppelin, the reargard plodded across the slope, each man roped to his neighbour for safety's sake. The Norwegians somewhere far above them were forgotten. Even if they had already rallied after that last attack, they could not harm the *Edelweiss* troopers; now the enemy was Nature itself. A false move could well endanger the whole group. Cautiously, in the lead, his nailed boots making a harsh squeaking noise which indicated to Stuermer that there was ice just beneath the surface of the new snow, the big colonel felt the way with his entrenching tool, using it as a kind of rudimentary ice-pick.

Greul's party had already safely negotiated the terrain for he could see the marks of their boots in the snow. They were somewhere beyond the slope out of sight.

Doggedly Stuermer and his little group plodded on, heads bent against the icy wind that had them continually blinking back their tears. Stuermer was certain they were crossing a kind of glacier which had been recently covered by the new snow; the cold was too intense for an ordinary snowfield. He began to zig-zag for extra safety, though the backs of his legs immediately started to scream in agony at the effort of bending his body at that unnatural angle. In spite of the wind, men's bodies dripped with sweat at the exertion – and the tension. They didn't need to be told why their colonel was imposing this extra effort on them for they were all veteran climbers. They knew they were on a glacier and they knew the dangers. The slick surface, the sudden change in the direction of the wind which might send an avalance speeding down it at a hundred kilometres an hour, the thin snow covering a limitless crevasse . . . No mountaineer worth his salt fooled with a glacier.

Now they were advancing at a snail's pace, with Stuermer prodding each fresh step with his entrenching tool, racked with an agony of indecision. What lay below the snow . . .? Ice again. *Or nothing?*

Twice they came across fissures in the snow with nothing beneath and each time Stuermer had to make himself be the first to jump them, while the man hung back on the rope grimly, knowing that the ice on the far side might not hold his weight and he could fall hundreds of metres to his death or, worse, an icy prison cell where he would die slowly in frozen misery. Both times the ice held. Once, too, he had been forced to stretch out across a particularly large hole in the glacier, turning himself into a human bridge, while his men crawled across his outstretched body and he had felt his tormented burning limbs could not bear the strain an instant more.

It was just after they had spotted Major Greul's party waiting for them beyond a rise and, further off, the coastal road with what appeared to be a large section of men moving along it, that it happened. Totally without warning, the ground slipped from beneath Stuermer's feet. The shovel flew from his hand. He tried to grab hold. In vain. He was falling at a tremendous rate. Involuntarily, a scream of fear was ripped from his mouth. Just in time, he prevented himself from soiling his trousers at the thought that he was falling to his death.

Suddenly the rope cut into his stomach cruelly and he gasped with shock. His tremendous fall ceased abruptly and his body was swung outwards and smacked hard into the surface of the rock. Stuermer blacked out momentarily. When he came to, he found himself gasping for breath like some ancient asthmatic. If he didn't act, he told himself, still trying to fight off the blackness which threatened to overwhelm him, he'd black out again – and that would be fatal. Acting instinctively, he reached out his bleeding, battered hand and found the Prusik sling which he carried in his belt. As hastily as he could with his frozen, torn fingers, he fitted it and placed his right foot in the stirrup. He sighed with relief. The killing pressure on his waist had been relieved. He took a deep breath of icy air of the chamber which sliced his lungs like the blade of a sharp knife.

'Sir,' Ox-Jo's voice floated down faintly from far above. 'Do you hear me . . . sir?'

Stuermer craned his neck in the silvery, icy gloom. He could just make out the lighter patch of the exit to the fissure but he couldn't see Ox-Jo. He must be the full extent of the rope down. That meant, he did a quick calculation, five metres between each man . . . twenty men at least in his party . . . at least one hundred metres down. He knew in a moment Ox-Jo would suggest he and the rest would haul him up by the rope, but he knew, too, he couldn't chance having the rope sawn through by the sharp rocks inside the chasm. His luck wouldn't hold a second time.

'Listen,' he cried, his voice echoing strangely in that narrow chamber of rock and ice. 'Don't try to pull me up . . . I'll make it myself. I'll use the rope as far as it goes . . . then I'll climb the rest . . . Understood?'

There was a moment's hesitation from above. 'Understood, sir,' Ox-Jo's voice came floating down again and Stuermer seemed to sense the disquiet in it. But there was no time to worry about Ox-Jo's feelings now. The icy cold was already beginning to pinch cruelly at his fingers and feet. Soon, if he didn't move, he would be too paralysed to attempt the climb, which was going to be damnably difficult as it was anyway. 'Right,' he commanded himself, 'start, man!' He reached up and grabbed the rope above his head.

'*Huns!*' Major Ferguson breathed, swinging his binoculars round and viewing the tiny figures scattered over the snowfield, clearly outlined against the background of glittering white.

Sergeant-Major MacDonald, crouching next to him on the side of the coastal road, caught his breath and felt the same excitement he had experienced that day in March 1918 when the Germans came stolidly across no-man's-land, in perfect formation with their brass bands playing military marches – that was until the Guards' machine guns had started to chatter. 'All of you,' he commanded, without taking his eyes off the Germans nearly a mile away, 'put one up the spout and click yer safety catches off!'

The old familiar sound of bolts being drawn back and bullets being inserted had a new dimension this afternoon, he told himself. He could even feel his hands trembling slightly. He chided himself that he was acting like a silly little kid getting his first smell of a woman on heat.

His lips moving, Major Ferguson counted the Germans, grouped in two parties, one further down the slope, the other higher up and clustered together in a decidedly unmilitary-looking sort of formation. There were about one hundred of them; he outnumbered them two to one. But where were the Norwegians? Were there other Germans beyond the height, who were still occupied fighting the Norwegians they had heard firing earlier? He bit his bottom lip. He didn't know the answer to that one. What was he to do? Tackle this lot or move onto the railway line which couldn't be more than a couple of miles away now? Abruptly the Germans made up his mind for him. Suddenly a signal flare curved into the grey sky, exploded with a slight crack and hung there menacingly, the faces of the men upturned to stare at it, a sickly green hue.

'What's that in aid of, sir?' MacDonald asked, puzzled.

'Recognition. They're not sure who we are, MacDonald. After all, they have other troops down in Narvik itself. Come on, we've got a few minutes left before they spot us for what we are.' He tugged out his own bell-shaped flare pistol, inserted a green flare and, holding it above his head, fired, while MacDonald got the men together, their exhaustion completely vanished now. 'All right men,' Ferguson, cried excitedly, his blood racing at the prospect of action, 'at the double and keep yer heads down! They'll be firing at us soon. *Move!*'

Ducked low, their rifles at the trail, the Guardsmen started to double forward, as the first startled slugs began to wing their way.

Down deep in the fissure Colonel Stuermer did not hear the first snap-and-crackle of rifle-fire as the men of Major Greul's group discovered the sudden presence of the enemy. The only sound he heard was the ominous groaning of the century-old ice all around him and his own harsh laboured breathing, as he fought his lone battle against Nature.

Hand over hand, the muscles of his arms and legs blazing with murderous pain, he climbed ever upwards, forcing himself to control his movements so that he didn't cause the rope upon which his life now hung to fray unnecessarily. More than once, he felt the strength seem to slip from his tall, lean body. He was tempted to let go, let Nature have its way, surrender to that awesome pain for good. Yet somehow he managed to fight the temptation off and continue.

As he climbed, he knew that soon he would bump into rock. These fissures were always the same, like a bottle, broad at the bottom, narrow at the top. With luck he'd reach the narrow funnel of the top before the rope went, then he'd abandon it and continue upwards by leverage up the rock wall. *With luck*, a cynical little voice said at the back of his mind. He ignored it. There was nothing he could do. He continued his snail's pace upwards.

Suddenly, after he had been climbing for perhaps ten minutes, there was a slight jerk on the rope. He felt it slacken for an instant and then tighten again. He sensed the thrill of fear which ran through his big body. He knew what it meant. *The rope was beginning to fray!*

He stopped and hung there. Desperately he peered upwards, but he could see little in that grey opaque light. Should he leave the rope now? He'd need every last bit of strength for the rock climb. The rope trembled again, more violently. Gingerly he advanced a little further, knowing he would have to abandon it soon. *Yes*, the cruel voice at the back of his brain sneered, *before it abandons you, comrade!* A sharp crack alerted his every sense. It was going now. He flung up his left hand. It hit rock. It was now or never. In the same instant that the rope went, he slammed his feet backwards and hit the rock wall, flinging his hands outwards simultaneously, and found a finger-hold. *God in heaven*, the little voice said in admiration this time, *you have the luck of the saints!*

For a long minute he hung there, gasping with relief after the strain of the rope, not feeling the icy sharp rocks that were cutting at his fingers. But he knew he soon would and he had to be on his way again. First, however, he must turn round and use his powerful shoulder muscles as his main means of propulsion. Gently he released one hand from the rock face and instantly felt the shudder of violent pain run throughout his spread-out body as the hand took the whole strain. Grimly he dug his boots in, and let go of the other hand. For one horrifying moment, he sensed himself hovering there in mid-air with no support, about to plummet to his death on the rock floor below, and then, like a professional acrobat, he had swung round and felt the comforting slap of the rock face against his shoulders. He had done it! He was ready for the last stage!

Ten minutes later, he had reached the top, ears already filled with the hysterical hiss of machine gun fire and the dry snap of rifles answering back. Willing hands helped him out and he fell flat on his face in the snow, shaking like a leaf, heart pounding away furiously, as if it might well break out of his ribcage at any moment, knowing even as he lay there, he had to start issuing orders, getting the men moving again down to that damned railway line before it was too late . . .

# *BOOK THREE: THE LAST BATTLE*

# ONE

The bitter wind had stopped now, but it was still snowing steadily. Below the main deck of the troopship there was the jingle of mess tins and knives and forks as the sailors, their duty done, lined up for their favourite breakfast 'snorkers and cowboy beans'. There would be enough, more than enough, for the crew; the 'brown jobs', as the sailors called them, had had no appetite for a big breakfast. They were going into action for the very first time and their minds were on other things than sausages and beans.

Now they lined up, pink-faced and chilled, gripped by tension, which seemed to slow them down, make their every movement sluggish and half-hearted. Even the NCOs pacing up and down the well-scrubbed deck, cleaned now of the night's vomit, were without spirit, their commands soft and lacking the usual harsh military precision. As for the officers, all of them without exception, clerks and storekeepers a mere six months before, they stood in small groups, smoking listlessly, hardly exchanging a word with each other, all waiting for what was soon to come.

It came with startling suddenness. As if some invisible hand had thrown a gigantic power switch, a tremendous flash of brilliant purple light split the grey, leaden sky. The men waiting to go over the side cowered instinctively. Then it commenced, the naval bombardment which their officers had promised would 'soften up the Jerries'. The naval guns roared and, even at that distance from the *Warspite*, they could feel the hot, damp slap of the 15-inch cannon washing their frozen pink faces. Chicago pianos chattered. Tracer, red, green, white, zipped across the water into Narvik, gaining speed by the instant.

Everywhere on the German-held coast signal flares hushed into the grey sky, as the God of War drew his first fiery breath.

'*Stand by!*' the officers called and shrilled their whistles.

'*Stand by to get into the boats!*' the NCOs echoed.

'*Move!*' the company commanders yelled.

'*Right smartish now!*' the NCOs bellowed.

Even before they knew what was happening, the heavily-laden Territorials were tumbling over the side, being screamed at here and there as they lost their balance and fell or let their rifles fall from nerveless fingers, clambering into the waiting boats. On the shore the Germans waited.

'All right, me lucky lads!' the matelots cried, as the Navy men at the oars took the strain, 'put yer backs into it! Let's get rid of these sodding brown chaps right quick and get back to housey-housey!'

And on the upper deck, the general turned his back on the captain and had a quick pull at the little silver, leather-bound flask of whisky. For better or worse he had done it. He had sent them on their way. The attack on Narvik was beginning.

'*Achtung!*' the German NCOs bellowed, raising their right hands, as if they were back on the peacetime ranges at *Sennelager* and the crews bore white cloth numerals on their backs indicating their positions at the gun – gun-layer, number two, commander etc. – so that the watching umpires could see at a glance that each man was carrying out his task correctly. '*FEUER!*'

The little portable mountain howitzers erupted, slamming back from their mountings, steaming yellow shell-cases tumbling from their suddenly open breeches. Abruptly, spouts of whirling white water flecked the sombre green of the fiord and, here and there, a boat disappeared from view for an instant.

Higher up, General Dietl focused his glasses hastily.

The whole narrow stretch of water seemed filled with rowing boats. The Tommies had finally acted. This was it, the full-scale invasion of Narvik. He ducked instinctively as a salvo of 15-inch shells from the *Warspite*, out there somewhere in the fog of war, went roaring overhead in a tremendous *whoosh*, like an express hurtling through a provincial station.

Next to him an officer said in a quavering voice, 'My God, sir, they're throwing everything at us – except the shitting kitchen sink!'

Dietl opened his mouth to tell the young officer that he had once said the same thing back on the Piave in Italy in '17. Next moment, an Italian kitchen sink *had* come flying through the air to land only metres from his own particular funk-hole. Then he thought better of it; one shouldn't tempt the fates. 'It's the real thing now, *meine Herren*,' he announced instead, lowering his glasses. 'They're coming in in force. My guess is that they've got a whole brigade of infantry out there.'

'Holy strawsack!' someone groaned at the news and then gasped, as a salvo of the *Warspite*'s shells slammed into a position held by the sailors from one of the sunken destroyers. They disappeared in a fury of black smoke and scarlet flame as if they had never even been there. The pathetic few cannon in the possession of the mountaineers didn't stand a chance against the English warship's tremendous guns. They would grind the mountain howitzers into the ground before the hour was out. The question now was whether Dietl's two thousand *Jager*, plus the thousand-odd sailors who were not trained for land warfare, would suffer the same fate. It was a question that General Dietl attempted to answer as the invasion fleet came ever nearer.

'I think, gentlemen,' he said raising his voice over the gunfire, 'we cannot attempt to defend everything. As always the old Prussian motto *klotzen nicht kleckern*[1]

[1] Roughly, 'Mass and not scatter'.

applies. He who attempts to defend everything, defends nothing in the end.'

There was a murmur of agreement from his officers, but they didn't take their eyes off the mass of boats getting ever closer and the whirling spouts of water that erupted in between at regular intervals, though the fire of the little howitzers was becoming noticeably weaker as the enemy guns zeroed in on the mountaineers.

'Once they have pierced the outer skin of our defences, wherever that may be, I shall withdraw the men from the eastern suburbs of Narvik and group in the west running out along the Robakfiord. I don't want to give them a chance of turning my flank there or cutting us off entirely if the worst comes to the worst.'

He did not say what that eventuality might be, but he did not need to. His officers knew it already. A retreat to the railway line and, if the enemy broke through there, the final disgrace, withdrawal into Sweden and internment.

'Sir,' someone broke the silence in the room overlooking the fiord, 'they've got another 75mm.'

Dietl nodded as if it were only of academic interest that another of his few remaining guns had been knocked out. 'Of course,' he continued, 'we know that they have a raiding party out to our rear. What we don't know is just how big that English group is.' He sucked his teeth and frowned, as if he had just discovered a cavity in one of them. 'Is it just a reconnaissance force or is it going to be a determined attempt to cut off our rear? And I don't have to tell you what that would mean?' He did though. 'We would be forced to evacuate Narvik and group on the railway line. Damn and blast it all,' he said with sudden venom, 'I wish I'd never heard of that damned railway line! It's hampering my whole tactical thinking.' He calmed down almost immediately and watched as yet another howitzer disappeared in a vicious spurt of red flame, its crew, dark little objects whirling upwards momentarily, a frenzy of flailing, severed limbs. 'If only

I knew that Stuermer's *Edelweiss* was out there to my rear,' he said almost to himself. Then his voice picked up again and he reached for his helmet, hanging on a peg in what had once been the living room of a Norwegian fish merchant. 'Come, gentlemen, I think it is time to go to the war. The English are about to arrive on our shores and it would not be polite if we failed to be there to welcome them.'

No one laughed.

'All right, me lucky lads, out yer go. Yer won't even get yer plates o' meat wet!' the sailors said, as the first enemy bullets started to pluck at the water all around them.

'Bollocks!' the soldiers cried back, and, 'I don't think I like the kind of welcome old Jerry's giving us!'

'What did yer expect, Snow Bleeding White and the Bleeding Seven Dwarfs!' the sailors mocked.

Then the heavily laden soldiers were plunging over the side up to their knees in the icy water, stumbling and falling, picking themselves up again and running as best they could for the timbered jetties, the German machine gun on their left flank ripping the length of the assault-line. A motorboat was hit. It burst into flames immediately. Sailors and soldiers, the quick and the dead, were flung into the sea in crazy promiscuity. The wounded screamed for help, mother, God. Men choked and coughed, black-faced and panicked, as the escaping diesel oil filled their lungs. Some just rolled from side to side in the faint tide, heads lolled to one side obscenely.

But now the first soldiers were running crouched along the timber jetty, bunched badly, poorly trained as they were, but with enough courage and determination to send the mountaineers in their peaked caps reeling back. A grenade sailed through the air and exploded right on top of the machine gun nest which was holding up the bulk of the advance. One of the gunners' heads, complete with cap, rolled along the jetty like an abandoned football.

The Terriers charged on, long heavy bayonets flashing, carried away by the bloodlust of war now, neither giving nor expecting quarter. A sailor with floppy cap and long flowing black ribbons dropped his rifle and raised his hands in surrender. '*Kamerad!*' he cried piteously, '*kamerad!*'

They knew what it meant; they'd heard the word from their fathers' tales of the Old War. But it didn't stop them. Half a dozen bayonets flashed. Men grunted and withdrew their weapons with a terrible sucking noise. The German sailor crumpled under the feet of those who followed.

Another group of German sailors was overrun. They suffered the same fate. The Terriers were crazy by now. They smashed their brass-shod butts down on the dying faces of the sailors, turning them into a red bubbling gore through which the bones gleamed a brilliant, startling white.

Into a stone house which was a German strongpoint. The enemy fled firing upstairs, but nothing could stop the Terriers now. One of them scaled the outside wall, a sack of grenades around his neck, ignoring the slugs chipping off little bits of stone all around and showering his face with splinters. He clambered on to the flat roof and raised his thumbs in a sign of triumph.

'That's the stuff to give the troops, Geordie!' his mates roared above the racket, the sweat streaming down their faces.

The soldier pulled out the pins of three grenades and flung them down the chimney. The walls erupted outwards and thick smoke poured from every crack. A kind of smoke signal rose from the chimney. Then, as the Geordie fell dead, caught neatly in the forehead by a sniper's bullet, the survivors, screaming and terrified, faces black with smoke, their uniforms smouldering and tattered, came staggering out to be mown down mercilessly.

But now too many of the sailors, poorly trained and very scared, were surrendering, all to be shot. Suddenly the madness went out of the Terriers. They blinked their eyes and tried to control their hectic, harsh breathing, as if waking up from a bad dream. The bloodlust left them. Abruptly, they felt weak and groggy, hardly strong enough to disarm the Germans. Some looked back along the jetty behind them, seemingly surprised at the corpses, Germans and Terriers, which littered it in ungainly lumps, as if they could not believe the evidence of their own eyes. A few leaned against the timbered walls of the houses and began to vomit. It was all over. They had had their first taste of battle. They had been blooded . . .

Back in the wardroom, the general raised his glass of brandy somewhat shakily in acknowledgement to his staff and the naval officers present. 'Thank you, gentlemen. The troops have done us proud . . . I knew they wouldn't let us down.' He beamed at the naval officers sipping their pink gins and feeling a little out of it. 'I know you gentlemen of the Navy thought we – er pongoes,' he used his newly acquired word carefully, 'might not pull it off. After all, we are most of us weekend soldiers. But we did, didn't we? The Boche have evacuated the eastern suburbs altogether and the way my brigade is keeping up the pressure, I can't—'

'Sir,' an excited voice cut into his little speech.

He turned around, annoyed. He knew what the naval types had been saying about him behind his back before the landing; he was savouring this moment. It was Jenkins, his chief signals officer. 'What is it, Jenkins?' he snapped with irritation. Jenkins wore glasses and he had never much gone on officers who wore glasses for some reason he could not quite define.

'Urgent, sir . . . Sorry to trouble, you . . . Thought it justified doing so, sir . . . It's from Ferguson . . .' Jenkins always spoke in quick excited bursts, as if he were one of his own signals. He thrust the buff-coloured message form at the general.

The brigade commander accepted it, the brandy still in his right hand, awkwardly. For a moment he thought he'd give Jenkins the glass to hold, then he changed his mind. He might need the fortification alcohol offered. He downed it in one go and read the message, holding it away from him in order to see the print. Then he read it again for the benefit of the others and also to give himself time to make up his mind what it meant and its significance for the attack on Narvik. 'Beg to report . . . in contact with the enemy since twenty hundred hours 15 April . . . approx. position . . . Signal Box 20 . . . Ferguson, Major, Scots Guards . . .' He stopped suddenly, as it finally dawned on him what the message meant. Ferguson hadn't carried out the original plan at all. 'Signal Box Twenty' meant he was on the railway line running to Sweden! The arrogant Scots aristocrat, who thought him a fumbling, bumbling Colonel Blimp who should never have been given an active command, had gone and got himself involved in a completely different operation. His face began to flush angrily and he was just about to burst into an angry condemnation of the Guardee when he saw the looks on the faces of the officers all around him, even those of the naval types who couldn't be expected to understand much about land tactics. They were all beginning to smile and nod significantly, as if the message had been good news.

His chief-of-staff, who was the only other regular army officer present, raised his glass, as if in a toast. 'I think that calls for another drink, sir, don't you?' he said in his usual brisk fashion. 'Steward – another chota peg.'

Slightly bewildered, the general let his glass be filled too with the rest, waiting for his chief-of-staff to enlighten him.

'Well, Laird of the Seven Lochs, wherever you may be this night, here's to you and yours!' the chief said solemnly. 'Now you'll certainly have the Boche pulling out of Narvik for us, though I'm afraid you have bitten off a bit more than you can chew. Down the hatch, gentlemen!'

Obediently, they did as they were commanded, including the general, who was still trying to comprehend what his chief had meant . . .

## TWO

'Will the big stupid bastards never give up!' Ox-Jo groaned, as the big Guardsmen started to lumber forward once again, bayonets fixed, coming out of the snow on both sides of the rail track. 'Don't they shitting well know when they've had enough!'

'By the docked dick of the Great Rabbi!' Jap cursed angrily, and flung himself down yet once again on the cartridge-littered floor of the little signal house. 'I can't shitting well see straight, I'm so tired.' He pressed the butt of his carbine into his shoulder and waited. Ammunition was running low, the CO had said; they couldn't afford to waste it. As soon as they broke into a final run and started shouting he would fire . . . not before.

All around him the weary defenders did the same, even the lightly wounded who were manning the posts left abandoned by the dead now, for every man was needed in the firing line.

'*Scotland fer ever . . . come awa, Jimmy!*' The strange barbaric cries came floating over the couple of hundred metres of ground that separated the two forces.

'Stand by to fire,' Stuermer rapped. He was kneeling on the floor, his mountain knife forced in between the teeth of a dying boy writhing in agony among the cartridge cases, so that he wouldn't bite off his tongue. The boy started to grind his teeth on the blade and twitch convulsively, as if he were having a fit. He would be dead in a matter of minutes, Stuermer knew. 'Don't waste a single round, do you hear?'

At his feet the boy bit hard at the knife, his spine curving in absolute mortal agony, almost tearing the blade out of Stuermer's hand in his final dying paroxysm, then he fell back and Stuermer was hastening to sprawl next to Greul in the firing line as the Scots began their crazy, brave assault.

The red-haired officer in front of the attacking soldiers seemed to bear a charmed life. He was minus his helmet, blood trickling down the side of his face, as he led the attack along the left side of the railway line, machine gun clutched tightly to his side, coolly directing its fire to left and right, as if he were back on some peacetime firing range.

Greul watched the Englishman, noting with admiration how skilfully he led his troops and with what bravery. Suddenly he felt a sense of identification. The tall, red-haired Englishman could have been himself, as he urged his men on, waving his free hand, shouting encouragement, turning his back time and time again to the men in the signal box, as if he were utterly contemptuous of their fire. 'That Englishman should have been one of us, sir,' he yelled, 'a German!'

'What did you say?' Stuermer asked, taking careful aim at the man, knowing that when they did open fire, he'd take him out. That might well take the steam out of their attack. All day the English had been attacking, ever since they had beaten them in the race for the railway line and their superior strength was beginning to tell, especially since they had been reinforced by the Norwegians two hours before. It was Stuermer's guess that his little force was at present outnumbered four to one, and he needed all the help he could get to survive the night. Thus he determined he would make a personal target of the enemy's red-haired commander. It was something he disliked doing. In their big spell of combat in Poland the previous year, he had pretended to himself that the men he had been forced to kill had been chosen at random; that he had not picked them personally to die. This time it would be different. He lined up the running man in his sight, waiting for the right moment, forcing himself to breathe regularly, as he started that fatal last squeeze.

But the Laird of the Seven Lochs was not fated to die – just yet. In the same instant that Stuermer pressed his trigger, Jap screamed from the other side of the room, 'The Norwegians – they're coming in from the ditch – *with fire bombs!*'

Stuermer's slug went hopelessly wild. Next moment he had doubled across the room, the slugs slamming into the walls on all sides, as the English intensified their attack, obviously to cover the Norwegians' assault from the ditch to the right of the building. He flung himself down next to Jap and peered through the ragged hole in the wall.

Fifty Norwegians were rushing their position. Some carried their rifles at the trail, ready for action, but most had them slung over their shoulders, bombs clutched in both hands.

'God, you're right,' Stuermer yelled and cried, 'fire . . . knock the bombers . . .'

The rest of his command was drowned as Jap's position erupted. A Norwegian went down and his bomb exploded beneath his falling body. Next instant he was a mass of fire, the snow hissing angrily and retreating from the searing flame. Another went reeling away, blood jetting from a shattered arm. 'That shit won't be throwing any more bombs!' Jap said grimly and thrust home a fresh magazine. But still the Norwegians kept on coming, as the frantic *Edelweiss* pumped their bolts, trying to keep them from reaching throwing distance. But that wasn't to be. As another Norwegian fell screaming on his own bomb which, erupting into flame, turned him into a fiery torch, Stuermer knew that this time they were not going to be able to beat off the concerted attack. This time the enemy would surely burn them out. He had to get the men out while there was still time. 'Greul,' he yelled at the big major at the other side of the room, 'keep them off another five minutes. Break off the action then and beat it downstairs. I'll be waiting to give you cover!'

'But, sir . . .'

Stuermer was not listening. Motioning to Jap to follow him, he was already running for the stairs. He took them at a run and tried not to see the dead mountaineers who packed the bottom floor. Here, in what had once been the station-master's kitchen, they were still relatively protected from the enemy's attack, for the place was situated in dead ground. Desperately he paused there among his dead soldiers, trying not to look at their eyes which seemed at that moment to stare up at him as if in accusation, casting around for a way out of the trap.

'We're at the end of a row of cottages, sir,' Jap said, as if reading the big colonel's mind. 'Must have been lived in by railway workers or something. I had a quick look at them when we first got here, sir – for military reasons, of course,' he added hastily and looked down at his hands.

Stuermer forced a grin in spite of the tight situation they were in. 'You and military reasons! More like *sauce* reasons for you and that big rogue up there, I'll be bound.'

'Mean shits,' Jap said unperturbed, 'these Norwegians. Didn't even leave a bottle of beer behind when they took . . .'

The first panicky yell came from upstairs as a fire bomb exploded on the roof with a great *whoosh*. Most of the station-master's place was made of wood. So it wouldn't be long before it was burning fiercely. The thought added a new urgency to the problem of escape. 'Standard street fighting technique, eh, Jap?' Stuermer said hastily. 'Mousehole through that wall into the next place and then into the next, keep fighting them off all the time until the . . .'

'. . . the shitting steam goes out of their attack.' Jap completed the sentence for him, 'God willing!' Jap crossed himself in the elaborate Bavarian fashion, though the only time he ever went into a church was when he wanted to steal something to pay for drink.

'You've got it, Jap. Get your section down here and let's get damned well started while there's still time.' Not waiting for Jap to obey, he pulled out the bayonet from the scabbard of one of the dead mountaineers and began scratching away at the poor wattle and cement construction, his ears already picking up the first dread sound of wood beginning to burn above . . .

'Blast and damn!' Major Ferguson yelled, staggered, and almost dropped his smoking Tommy-gun, 'the buggers have gone and shot me!'

MacDonald, the perfect senior noncom, always there when needed, caught the swaying major and looked down at the officer's left hand. There was a deep gouge along the back of his hand, from which welled thick dark blood, looking like the juice of an overripe crushed fig. 'Not too bad, sir,' he said, pulling out his yellow wound bandage, opening it swiftly and pressing the pad itself on the wound before swiftly tying the brown bandage around the hand.

Now that the major had been hit and stopped, the men were going to ground, taking cover where they could and firing at the high house, its roof already beginning to burn where the fire bombs had penetrated the thick snow. MacDonald nodded his approval. The lads had already done enough. Let the 'Norgies', as they were now calling their new allies, do the rest. It was their sodding country, after all. Let them suffer a few dead for it.

'Must get on,' Ferguson said thickly, feeling a little nauseated but telling himself it was shock. He had felt the same way in '37 when a Pathan bullet, fired from one of their ancient muskets, thank God, had slammed into his chest at fifty yards' range. 'Can't slacken now . . . One last effort.' His Tommy-gun tumbled from suddenly nerveless fingers and he knew he had to sit down.

Gently, the giant NCO lowered him to the snow. 'Everything's going all right, sir,' he reassured the pale-faced officer, as the blood drained from his face, 'the Jerries have had it. That house is burning like a bonfire on Guy Fawkes' Night. They'll either come out with their hands up soon, or they'll end up like a lot of burned bangers.'

He took his eyes off the officer for a moment and stared at the house, with the smoke drifting thick and black from the oil in the bombs from its roof, while the Norwegians, carried away by their triumph and forgetful of their casualties, rushed the place once again, throwing their bombs before dropping, either dead or to take cover into the snow among the corpses which littered it everywhere. 'Poor sods,' he whispered under his breath, feeling momentarily sorry for the Jerries. He had seen what fire could do to a man when the Jerries had attacked with flamethrowers back in the trenches. It wasn't a pleasant sight.

Groggily, Ferguson struggled to his feet, shaking his head to fight off his nausea. 'All right, Sarnt-Major, get the men moving again. We want to be in at the kill, you know.'

'And win a sodding medal as well, I suppose,' MacDonald said scornfully under his breath. To Ferguson's face, he snapped militarily precise. 'Yessir . . . As you wish, *sir!*' and, raising his bayonet, cried above the crackle of the flames, 'Now come on you idle men, let's be having yer, you shower . . .'

Wearily the Jocks rose to their feet and shambled forward. 'Scotland for ever!' they cried hoarsely and stumbled into the smoke once more.

Stuermer, bare-headed, filthy, covered in smoke and brick dust, dropped lightly to the snow from the wall, Schmeisser clutched at the ready. Behind him, further up the row of houses, the station-master's place was burning fiercely, throwing up great clouds of smoke for which he was grateful. It covered him and his men. Soon, however, the enemy would be bold enough to enter the burning place and find out why no fire was coming from there any more; for now it was garrisoned solely by dead men.

Behind him, more and more of his troopers started to crawl out of the hole they had tunnelled in the wall of the last house and spread out, weapons at the ready. Stuermer licked his parched lips and wished he could swallow some of the snow, but he knew that would be unwise. He had enough trouble on his hands at the moment, without a bad case of the 'shits'.

Still crouched low, his heart thumping like a trip-hammer with excitement and tension, he crossed the little snow-covered road that ran along the railway line, his ears only half taking in the strange humming noise that came from the tracks, gaze fixed totally on the burning building.

Soon it would be night. Under the cover of darkness they could probably make a fighting retreat in the direction of Narvik; but would the men, exhausted from the events of the last few days and quite a few of them now wounded, be able to stick out a night retreat in sub-zero temperatures?

Behind him Major Greul obviously did not think so, for he was already organizing a perimeter defence around the last hut, knowing that the enemy would soon discover their escape from the station-master's house.

Stuermer frowned. What was he to do? The strange humming noise was becoming ever louder. It vaguely irritated him although he didn't know why.

Ox-Jo loomed up out of the growing gloom, a nasty gash down the side of his dirty, sweaty face. 'I've been up front, sir,' he said and wiped his scummed lips, as if he, too, was very thirsty. 'Those big buck-teethed Tommies under that red-haired officer are moving forward again.' He whipped a square-shaped tin from behind his back and offered it to Stuermer as if it were a royal present.

'One of them didn't quite make it, so I don't suppose he'll be needing this anymore.'

Stuermer took it and peered at the English words in the gloom. 'Corned-beef, produced in Argentina,' he read, and grinned. 'You searched him for other things, I take it?'

'I thought all those Englishmen in skirts drank whisky for breakfast,' he growled and wiped his lips again. 'But nary a drop on him. Mean shit!' he added, unfeelingly, about the Englishman he had just stabbed to death with his bayonet so that the noise of firing wouldn't give his hiding-place away.

Stuermer was feeling in a kind of daze as he opened the tin and scooped out a handful of the meat and then passed the can over to Ox-Jo. Somehow he didn't seem able to think clearly, although the Englishmen would be on to them soon. Instead he ate the meat mechanically, not even tasting it, but knowing that he must force it down; he hadn't eaten all day. The drumming of the railway line below grew louder and louder. Still he appeared unable to identify the sound. His mind seemed incapable of functioning.

'Form up, yer bleeding Scottish shower,' a tremendous voice brought home the danger of their position. 'Or do yer want a sodding invitation from King George personal . . .'

'Ox, they're coming!' Stuermer gasped and flung away the rest of the meat.

'*Achtung . . . sie kommen!*' Greul cried behind him, soldier to the very last. '*Alles hort auf mein Kommando . . .*'

'*Scotland for ever!*' That old cry which they had come to hate and dread came floating their way from the direction of the burning station-master's house, followed by an order in Norwegian. The enemy had discovered that there were only dead men there and they were coming in for the kill.

But that was not to be. Just as the first of the big

Englishmen came lumbering out of the gloom and smoke of war, bayoneted rifle clenched to his waist, to go down hands grabbing the air, as if climbing the rungs of an invisible ladder, caught in that sudden burst of heavy German machine gun fire, the screeching ancient locomotive came roaring round the bend, the rails drumming mightily under the weight of the heavily-laden train it was drawing, the proud crooked-cross banner of the 'New Germany' fluttering boldly at its front . . .

# THREE

'And which can, may I be so bold as to ask, Sergeant-Major, has the cunt in it?' one of the *Edelweiss* troopers cracked the old joke as the hungry men clustered around the pile of cans in the snow which General Dietl had brought up personally.

Colonel Stuermer grinned wearily. 'Always the same old jokes with soldiers, isn't it, General. You'd think they'd dream up something else?' he said, as he followed the skinny, tall general into the log house, which was now his new headquarters.

'Soldiers haven't much imagination, in my opinion,' Dietl said in a tired voice, taking off his peaked cap and handing it to a waiting orderly. 'Perhaps it's good that they don't have – considering the life they are forced to lead.'

Stuermer nodded his agreement. The general seemed to have aged ten years since he had last seen him in far-off Kufstein. There were dark circles under his eyes and the eyes themselves had lost their hawklike keenness of the old days.

Outside, the men had broken open the cans with their bayonets and were shovelling the cold meat into their mouths just like that. Only Jap and Ox-Jo did not seem hungry. They supervised the distribution of the cans, silently passing a bottle that Ox had traded somewhere or other to one another for a drink, their every movement seemingly an effort. Stuermer closed the door of the house and told himself the men were beat. Indeed it seemed what was left of the Mountain Division was completely exhausted, the men unshaven, apathetic, a look in their faded eyes that said they might well just break down and begin to sob if someone uttered a harsh word.

'There's not much fight left in them,' Dietl said, as if to confirm Stuermer's opinion. 'They've been at it too long and there have been too many casualties.' He sat down heavily at the kitchen table which was now his desk. 'Thank God for that train. I don't think many of them would have been capable of marching up here.'

He indicated that Stuermer should take a seat on one of the hard kitchen chairs. Outside the men were drifting away to find some sort of shelter in the crowded hamlet for the night. Far away, where the sailors were now holding the railway huts in place of *Edelweiss*, there came the faint rumble of artillery. Stuermer told himself that the English had brought up guns.

'Is that why you evacuated Narvik, sir?' Stuermer asked, made slightly uneasy by the general's sudden silence. It was totally unlike the tall Austrian general; in the old days he had been a great talker – for a general. 'Because of the men?'

'No,' Dietl answered. 'I had a choice to make – the port or the railway line. I decided on the railway line. The port's no good anyway. The English have got it sewn up completely now.'

Once again there fell one of the general's strange silences. In the distance the English guns thundered. Stuermer wondered how long the sailors could hold; they weren't trained for that sort of thing. 'What will they – the English – do next, sir? Attack us up here?'

'Finally yes, Stuermer. But the English are a slow, methodical people. They like to take their time. It's all that tea they drink. It makes them sluggish.' Dietl grinned and Stuermer returned the grin. The general, he remembered, was a great wine drinker; he would look down on people who drank tea. 'All the same I do not underestimate them, Stuermer,' he continued. 'They'll come in due course.' He traced two lines in the dust on the top of the kitchen table. 'Presently I'm holding this line of the railway to a depth of five kilometres, between the pass there and the huts you defended. Effectively, I am denying it to the English. In addition,' his dirty fingernail ran the length of the other line, 'I am holding a position between the railway and the coast, thus cutting the two parts of the English force off from one another. You understand?'

'I understand, sir.'

'So they will try to break through the line up to the coast. That will be their first objective. Then they'll tackle the railway line in full strength. It would be the logical solution for any commander.'

Stuermer frowned. That solution didn't seem correct to him. If he were the commander of the English troops, who would be tired too, he'd push them up the railway line from both sides. They'd be able to use the trains as well. But he was too exhausted to object. All he wanted to do now was to sleep. 'And my orders, sir?' he asked, in an attempt to bring the discussion to an end.

Dietl forced another weary grin. 'To hit the hay, my dear Stuermer, and sleep the sleep of the just. I'm going to keep you here as my – hm – mobile reserve. Let the sailor-boys do a bit of fighting for a change, instead of playing around with their pretty boats and waterfront whores. *You're* due for a good rest and, believe me, you'll get it. The Tommies, as I know them, won't be here for a long time yet . . .'

But there General Dietl was going to be proved wrong.

'Call me Digger,' the elderly quartermaster with the three ribbons of the Old War on his chest said, 'cos I dig 'em up first and then I plant 'em again.' He grinned, showing a mouthful of cheap false teeth.

'What?' MacDonald said, looking up from his canteen of mutton stew and staring at the other man, not particularly interested. All around him in the makeshift sergeants' mess the brigade had already set up in the newly captured port, the headquarters staff were eating heartily, cracking the usual jokes, laughing easily and often as if this were a peacetime mess at Aldershot. There was even Norwegian beer.

'I'm in Graves, you see,' the quartermaster said and the smile vanished from his mouth. 'Somebody's got to do it, you know.' He saw that big Guards noncom did not understand and added quickly, 'I dig out the lads that have been hit and give 'em a proper burial. Digger, you get it?'

MacDonald pushed away his mutton stew. Surprisingly enough he hadn't much appetite. 'I get it,' he answered, wondering whether he should go and check the Jocks' billets but telling himself that the sailors who had evacuated them by sea and brought them back to Narvik would have seen them all right; matelots were always pretty good at organizing grub and kip.

'They tell me that your lot has left me a lot of work back up there on the railway,' Digger continued, taking a swig of the thin Norwegian beer. 'The trouble with Guardsmen is that they're so big and, yer know, it takes four men to get one man out, especially when they're big and heavy. Ay,' he shook his grizzled head like a man who is sorely tried, 'they keep me busy.'

Suddenly MacDonald had a vision of the fifty Jocks they had left up there dead, being buried by the old sod facing him, tossed into the lime pits like logs of useless wood; he had seen it all before in the trenches. Anger, unusual in such a well-disciplined man as he was normally, flared up. Abruptly he hated the talkative quartermaster and all the rest of these base wallahs, laughing and joking as if nobody was getting killed out there. He rose to his feet, stretching to his full magnificent height, moustache bristling, 'Shut your fucking stupid cakehole,' he bellowed, 'or I'll shut it for you!'

He pushed his chair back and a dead silence fell over the big room. At the table the quartermaster went red, then white. 'I didn't mean anything,' he stuttered, 'I know people don't like me . . .'

'*Shut up!*' MacDonald roared in that famous voice which had made many a new recruit pee himself on the square. Grabbing his peaked cap, he marched out, eyes fixed on some distant object, as if not deigning to see these puny men who stared up at his passing in open-mouthed awe.

It was bitterly cold outside and because it was dark and no one could see that he was an NCO in the Brigade of Guards, MacDonald turned up the collar of his greatcoat, but he didn't put his hands in his pockets, although he had no gloves – that would be going a bit too far.

Idly, if a sergeant-major in the Guards could ever be called idle, he strode through the shattered streets of the port, catching a glimpse of light here and there from the cellars to which most of the population and a lot of the soldiers, too – to judge by the urgent squeaking of bedsprings here and there – had retired. He grinned abruptly, his bad temper vanished as quickly as it had come. You couldn't stop the average British Tommy; he'd be able to get his end in in the middle of the ruddy Sahara. He thought of his dead Jocks back there in the snow with their bayoneted rifles stuck in the ground to mark their shallow graves in the iron-hard earth. They'd never get their end in ever again. His grin vanished and suddenly he wished he'd asked for the spirits rations to which he was entitled as a senior noncom in the makeshift mess. He'd dearly love to put a few stiff belts of whisky inside him at this moment and fall into his bunk dead drunk. But that wasn't to be. He strode on aimlessly.

It was the steady pace of the sentries' boots on the frozen snow and the blued-out lights of the khaki-coloured staff cars coming and going into the drive of the big waterfront house that awoke him to the fact that he was approaching Brigade HQ. Hastily, with a guilty look to left and right to see if anyone had already spotted his 'crime', he pulled down his greatcoat collar. No one had.

Sergeant-Major MacDonald breathed a sigh of relief. The last time he had been on a 'fizzer' had been in 1918 when he had been on fatigues, emptying the officers' latrine buckets, which had to be cleaned by burning every morning. Somehow or other he had managed to set fire to the fluid that the buckets contained as well as the faeces. The whole latrine had caught ablaze and burnt down to the ground. Thereafter for months, whenever the battalion met at mealtimes behind the line, they had stood up as one when he entered to call, '*Here comes the Jock who burned the officers' shithouse down!*' For a while he had feared that he would go through life being called 'Shithouse MacDonald'.

For a moment he paused and watched the sentries as best he could in the gloom. They had their greatcoat collars turned up which was against regulations when on duty, he noted automatically, but otherwise they were quite well turned out for men on active service. He nodded his approval and was about to set off and find his billet, when a familiar face was illuminated by one of the sentries' torches as he stopped a car entering the drive to check the occupants' identity. It was the Laird, Major Ferguson, whom he had last seen having his hand attended to at the port's field dressing station, with the MO fussing and clicking his tongue in an apprehensive manner, muttering that, 'These kind of wounds are not so simple as you seem to think, Major. I might well have to pass you on to the base hospital on board ship for further treatment.' Now it seemed that Major Ferguson had managed to talk himself out of that one.

MacDonald watched as the sentry flashed his torch on the car's other occupant and was surprised to see that it was a civilian, a middle-aged haughty looking bloke who looked as if he was accustomed to giving orders – and having them obeyed. He frowned and then the sentry was stepping back and raising his rifle in salute. The car disappeared inside and the barrier was going down again, leaving the NCO to wonder what that little lot was about . . .

*

'General, I am sorry to disturb you at this hour,' Major Ferguson said formally and the general knew instinctively that the arrogant Guardee wasn't sorry at all. It didn't mean a thing to him that he was disrupting the only quiet hour of the day when a chap, even if he were a general officer, had the right to have a nice stiff brandy-and-soda and a good cigar. But his chief-of-staff, who knew about such things, the cunning bugger, had told him that Ferguson had highly-placed friends at the War Office, so he put a good face on it, as Ferguson introduced his civilian companion as 'Professor-Doctor Freund', whatever a 'professor-doctor' was. The man looked a Hebrew to him, and wasn't the Hebrew in charge of the War Office enough – him and his damned Belisha beacons! Still, they shook hands and the Norwegian, or whatever he was, accepted the general's hand, as if he passed the time of day with British general officers constantly. The general concluded he was a cocky bugger.

'General,' the civilian said in accented but precise English, 'do you know that man in that picture?' He pointed at the large coloured painting on the wall behind the general.

He looked at it. A big man with puffy eyes and a dimple, his dark brown, thin hair combed down across his forehead a bit like that feller, Hitler's. 'Can't say I do!' he replied.

'That is Vidkun Quisling,' the Professor-Doctor said.

'Oh,' the general said, puzzled. 'I see.' But he didn't. He frowned at Ferguson with his thick bandaged hand, but the damned Guardee didn't help him out.

Instead the Professor-Doctor said, 'Mr Quisling is our local Hitler here in Norway. Now that the Germans have come, he wishes to take over the country.'

''Fraid I know nothing of politics,' the general said hastily. 'Leave that to the clever Johnies in London.'

The Professor-Doctor looked at him, as if he was one of his patients come in to explain that he had had an unpleasant little accident and now found himself to be

suffering from 'a social disease'. 'Before the war and the Germans came, Mr Quisling,' he said firmly, 'built his own National Socialist Party in Norway. Now the members of that Party are actively helping the Germans.'

'I don't quite see,' the general began, but the Professor-Doctor didn't give him a chance to continue.

'For some time I have been building up contacts within that Party. Indeed I have been a member of it myself since 1938.'

'How interesting,' the general said for want of anything better to say and Ferguson saw that it was time for him to step in before his new friend, whom he had discovered at the hospital which had been taken over by the brigade, put his foot in it. 'Sir, Professor-Doctor Freund is a convinced opponent of the Boche and the Nazi Party – for obvious reasons.'

The Professor-Doctor looked down at his hands modestly, as if he wanted no personal acclaim on account of his Jewishness.

'He has infiltrated the Norwegian Nazi Party to pass on intelligence to his own people about their doings. Indeed, he warned them – though they didn't take any notice of the information, unfortunately – that the garrison commander here in Narvik when the Germans landed was a member of Quisling's lot. No wonder he handed them the place on a silver platter. Now he has the complete details of their members who have retreated with the Germans into the hills where the railway to Sweden runs and, sir, he personally could get right to General Dietl's HQ without any difficulty whatsoever. The Norwegian Nazis and the Boche regard him as one of them.'

'General Dietl?' the general queried.

'The Boche commander.'

'Oh, I see . . . but really what has this got to do with our operations?'

Major Ferguson took a deep breath and began to tell him . . .

## FOUR

'Permission to speak, sir?' MacDonald said shakily, his mind not really taking in the astonishing plan that Major Ferguson had just outlined to him.

'Yes, Sarnt-Major, fire away,' Ferguson said in high good humour, now he'd talked that old buffoon of a brigade commander into it. Opposite him, Professor-Doctor Freund sat on a ration case smoking moodily through a long ivory cigarette-holder.

'If I understand correctly, this gentleman,' he indicated the doctor, 'is going to pass us through the enemy's lines so that we can make a strike at the Jerry HQ?'

'That's right,' Ferguson said, really not interested in the big NCO's problems; he had other things on his mind. They were going to set out at dawn. There was a lot to be done by then.

'But they'll shoot us if they catch us in civvies, sir,' MacDonald protested. 'They'll treat us as spies.'

'First, they won't catch us, Sarnt-Major,' Ferguson said slowly, as if explaining something to a particularly stupid child. MacDonald was a top-flight NCO, he told himself, but he was too much 'brigade', too wooden in his thinking, not really cut out for this kind of operation. 'Second, we won't be wearing civvies. We will be wearing the uniform of the Royal Norwegian Army, posing as defectors and pre-war followers of this turncoat chap Quisling.'

On the ration case, the Doctor nodded, as if giving the statement his personal approval.

'But we don't speak Norwegian, sir,' MacDonald said a little desperately.

'No, but Professor-Doctor Freund does. He'll see we get through.'

'But once the balloon goes up, sir, they'll know we're

British and then we'll be miles inside their lines. We don't stan . . .'

'Sarnt-Major,' Ferguson cut him off firmly, 'I've done this sort of thing a dozen or more times in Palestine with Wingate. We often went into Arab territory to take out some leading terrorist or other.' His eyes sparkled excitedly. 'Once you lop off the head, the trunk folds up and dies. Palestine proved that time and time again.'

'But these aren't wogs, sir, these are Jerries. And they won't be fooled so easily,' MacDonald protested hotly, but even as he blurted out the words, he knew Ferguson wasn't listening.

'Better see to the fellers, Sarnt-Major,' he said easily, obviously wanting to get on with his plans with the Professor-Doctor. 'The lorry from brigade with the uniforms should be arriving soon. You can sort them out so that the chaps look fairly presentable to a strange eye. You'll be good at that, I am sure.' He grinned suddenly.

MacDonald stiffened to attention and swung him a tremendous salute, his face wooden, but inside he raged. For the major he was just another body, a well-disciplined toy soldier who did as he was told and left the thinking to the officers, for that was what they were paid for.

He stumbled blindly into the snowstorm outside, burning with anger. 'Shit said the King, and a thousand arseholes bent and took the strain,' he muttered to himself through tightly clenched teeth as he battled his way against the snow to the men's billets. 'For in those days the word of the bloody King was law, *I don't think!*' Of course, Ferguson was bloody mad. He had to be to cook up a plan like that with that ruddy Yid sawbones.

In the trenches back in the Old War MacDonald had seen men go crackers under the strain of the lice, the rats, the rotten grub, the incessant barrages, the constant fear of sudden violent death, but it had always been a loud affair with lots of crying and shouting and struggling. With one exception. There'd been an old lance-sergeant in the battalion, an old sweat, who, they said, had fought at Spion Kop in the Boer War. He'd been a real loner, always keeping to himself, even in the trenches. Somehow or other he'd always manage to find a funk-hole just for himself, where he'd squat alone, smoking his old clay pipe and looking at nothing. But he was a brave one, won the Military Medal and bar, always volunteering like a shot when they wanted someone to go out into no-man's-land on a night patrol, the most unpleasant task of all in the trenches. Then they found out why. By chance the CO sprang a surprise inspection on the battalion and found the sarge in his funk-hole playing with 'me things', as he called them when they came to take him away. His 'things' were bits and pieces of human beings, which he had cut off dead Jerries and pickled in his daily rum ration. He told the astonished CO he was trying 'to make me own Jerry'. His face had been as calm as a duckpond, and when they came for him from the RAMC,[1] nothing showed in his eyes. There was no struggling and no straitjacket – nothing. The medics called it monomania, he was told later. Now as Sergeant MacDonald paused at the door of the Jocks' billets, the icy, snow-filled wind forgotten for a moment, he remembered the strange look on that old lance-sergeant's face twenty-two years before and told himself that it hadn't been much different from that on Ferguson's face just now. He, too, was suffering from monomania. The only difference was that this particular candidate for the looney bin had the fates of over a hundred young soldiers in his hands. *What was he to do?*

The trucks had dumped them just behind the British lines on the right flank of the brigade where the road was fringed by the beginning of the high Plateau. From there they had marched through the last hour of the night to the furthest British outpost manned by a bunch of scruffy unshaven Territorials in ill-fitting leather jerkins with

[1] Royal Army Medical Corps.

stocking caps on their heads, who had made pointed remarks on their appearance: 'Christ, why should Hitler tremble' and 'What kind of Fred Karnos are you, shower' and the like, until they learned that these strangely clad Guardsmen were going through enemy lines. Then they had shut up and moved away from the Guardsmen as if they had some weird contagious disease, as the latter had drunk their tea and eaten their corned beef sandwiches. The Terriers hadn't even looked up from their slit trenches when they had left up the trail, but peered down at their hands, as if they didn't want to acknowledge their parting; as if they were condemned men who might cast a fatal shadow. Sergeant-Major MacDonald, bringing up the rear, had grown even more depressed.

Now since first light they had been climbing steadily, the usual banal and lecherous chatter killed by the effort and the knowledge that they were behind enemy lines, that is, all of them save the major and the Professor-Doctor, wearing a white ski smock and smart peaked cap, plus nailed climbing boots. They talked all the time, obviously pleased they had penetrated the German lines so easily.

Bringing up the rear, chasing the laggards on, helping a man here and there, Sergeant-Major MacDonald frowned as he watched them. So far it had been all right, but anyone who knew anything about war knew that the frontline was always thinly held – the front was a pretty lonely place. It was when you started to approach the rear that the troops started to become thick on the ground – and they were heading, according to the major, directly for a divisional headquarters. Christ, he told himself in sudden alarm, if Jerry divisional headquarters were anything like those of the British Army, there'd be crimson-faced, fat-gutted majors and colonels all over the place!

It was two hours after dawn when they had their first alarm. Suddenly the Professor-Doctor halted, turned his head to the wind and barked in his excellent English, 'Down!'

The command was given with such authority that the Guardsmen didn't wait for the major, but dropped instinctively, fumbling with their safety catches and ready for trouble. Ferguson and the Professor-Doctor followed the next instant.

'What is it?' Ferguson asked a little annoyed.

'Ski troops,' the Norwegian answered. 'Look.'

Ferguson craned his neck. Four tiny dark figures were coming their way, gliding almost noiselessly over the gleaming new snow, carbines slung over their backs, obviously not expecting any trouble. With his good hand, Ferguson fumbled for his revolver.

The Norwegian stopped him hastily. 'No,' he said, 'we want prisoners. They'll give us the exact location of the famous General Dietl's headquarters.'

'I understand,' Ferguson said, 'but I don't want to be lumbered with prisoners afterwards.'

'You don't have to,' the Professor-Doctor answered, rising already to his feet, hands raised, 'there will be no *afterwards*.' Next moment he was calling to the ski patrol in fluent German and the startled mountaineers were heading his way.

Ferguson and the Norwegian doctor didn't ask any of the men to do their dirty work for them. All they wanted from the men was another revolver for the Norwegian. MacDonald handed his over silently and the Norwegian smiled and said, 'I hate Germans because what they are doing to my race.'

Then the two of them herded the scared, bewildered Germans to the side of the track, where a large naked rock jutted out of the snow. The Professor-Doctor said something to them in German and indicated they should turn their backs to him and kneel down. Then they started to wail and cry out, wringing their hands, pleading with the stern-faced Norwegian in their own language. But he was unmoved and finally they settled down, turned and knelt like dumb animals ready to meet their fate.

The Professor-Doctor nodded to Ferguson, and he indicated the two he would deal with with a jerk of his revolver.

MacDonald tensed. He had heard about things like this, from blokes who had served out East or against the Turks in the Old War, but he had never thought he would be party to anything of the kind. He knew he should open his mouth and protest, just as he should have done when Ferguson had made them leave Chapman and Maxwell behind after the landing, but he didn't.

With a steady hand, Ferguson pressed the muzzle of his revolver to the back of the first German's head, just below the right ear. His knuckles whitened. A little way off the Professor-Doctor did the same, his face as calm and as expressionless as Ferguson's. At exactly the same moment they both pressed their triggers. Someone cried out. The Germans screamed piteously. The backs of their heads disappeared in a welter of blood, as if someone had tapped a soft-boiled egg with a heavy spoon. They slammed to the ground, gore and blood staining the snow bright red everywhere. Then it was the turn of the last two.

Afterwards Ferguson thrust his revolver back into its canvas holster and said in a sort of jolly voice, 'Well, Professor, I suppose we have just committed a war crime, eh?'

The Professor-Doctor laughed.

On the second day they started to pass large numbers of German troops, many of them sailors who looked out of place in this remote area in the floppy caps and short black coats which gave them little protection against the biting wind. They didn't seem much surprised to see an armed body of Norwegian soldiers in their midst, especially when the Professor-Doctor spoke to them in their own language, with much heel-clicking and many 'Heil Hitlers'. After these encounters the Professor-Doctor would grin at Ferguson and say something like, 'The Germans are not a very profound people in spite of their composers and philosophers. They take things very much at their face value.'

Towards evening the Professor-Doctor led them to a scattered, tumbledown hill farm, set low on the ground with stone walls and a roof covered in sod. He told the Guardsmen that the farmer was one of Quisling's men and bred cattle up here in the summer.

'More like bleeding huskies!' MacDonald told himself sourly, as they waited in the freezing wind, while the Professor-Doctor approached the house by himself.

Ten minutes later he reappeared at the door of the miserable place, accompanied by a large skinny man with an ugly face wearing, surprisingly enough for a farmer, some sort of uniform complete with Sam-Browne and what looked like black riding breeches.

'Christ,' MacDonald cursed under his breath, 'it's old Adolf himself!'

The Professor-Doctor waved to the long barn and shouted in Norwegian for the sake of his companion that they should enter the place. Happy to be out of the wind, they filed inside and slumped wearily into the old straw that was matted with dried-up animal droppings and smelled strongly of urine. But the men were too tired and cold to care. They just slumped there in the muck, shivering violently, as if suffering from some kind of fever. MacDonald looked down at his Jocks and frowned. He knew he should start getting them organized, but he hadn't the heart. As for Ferguson, he seemed to have completely forgotten the duties of an officer towards his men after a long day's march – the inspection of feet and the usual routine of getting them fed and warmed. Instead he pored over his map with almost feverish intensity, his mouth moving, MacDonald noticed with an even deeper frown, for it was a bad sign, as he did so.

Half an hour later, the Professor-Doctor, smiles all over his sallow face, appeared at the door of the barn with two sturdy wenches in aprons and ankle-length black skirts and men's boots. They were lugging a great pail of peasoup between them, a sack containing round flat country loaves on their broad shoulders. They grinned shyly when the Guardsmen started to sit up and look up at them, then put their burdens down, curtsied, and were off like a flash, as if they half-expected the big soldiers to rape them in the straw there and then.

In high good humour, Professor-Doctor Freund spread his hands like a latterday Jesus about to feed the Multitude. 'Hot food, gentlemen,' he announced. 'I have fooled the farmer completely. Now eat.' With that he strode purposefully to an expectant Ferguson, while MacDonald roused himself from his lethargy and began to get the Guardsmen organized with their mess tins before the soup went cold.

They were munching happily on the last of the coarse brown bread, which was warm too, as if it had been freshly baked, though it did have what appeared to MacDonald to be bits of straw in it everywhere, occasionally belching and farting softly on account of the peas, when Ferguson called, 'Sarnt-Major, have the men pay attention.'

'Yes sir,' MacDonald jumped to his feet and said, 'all right, remain seated, but pay attention to the officer.'

He turned back to Ferguson and the Professor-Doctor who smiled knowingly, as if he was certain that they would be surprised at what would happen next. 'Men all present and correct, sir,' he said very formally.

'Thank you, Sergeant-Major,' Ferguson said with equal formality, as if this was an important occasion. He cleared his throat and began, 'Men, at dawn we go in . . .'

## FIVE

For a moment the dark clouds parted in the moon's path and the farmyard gleamed in the cold light. Ox-Jo's nostrils were assailed from the right by the acrid ammoniacal stench of animal piss. Then the moon was gone again and all was darkness, with no sound save the faint sigh of the wind. But that instant had sufficed for Ox-Jo. He had been able to spot the pig-sty, which was the reason that they had spent half the night up here in the hills away from HQ in temperatures which, according to Jap, would 'freeze the balls off'n a snowman' – if he had any. 'Come on, shithead,' he whispered urgently, clutching the precious bottle of schnapps. 'Let's get the lead out.' He licked his lips hungrily. 'I can just taste a great kilo chunk of roast pork going down my cakehole. Heaven, arse and cloudburst, I'll stuff myself with pork until I start grunting like one of the lovely little shits.'

'You always do,' Jap said unkindly. 'Did no one never tell yer? Let's get the porker first.' They crept forward.

It had all started the previous midday when once again the meal had consisted of tinned meat and a piece of black bread, washed down with lukewarm ersatz coffee made of acorns. Ox-Jo had exploded, pushing the tin canteen away from him in disgust, 'Christ, Old Man a shitting well agen! I can even taste their sweaty feet by now. They didn't wash 'em before they minced the old buggers up to make meat for the Greater German *Wehrmacht*.' He pulled an exceedingly sour face. 'Not even a canteen of suds – gnat's piss that it is – to wash the goo down with. Just this rotten nigger sweat they call coffee. What a shitting life!'

The outburst had been followed by a long sulky silence which lasted until Jap, sitting next to him at the trestle table, began to make little grunting noises. Ox-Jo looked at his running-mate sourly. 'And what's up with you, you little yellow turd? Ain't yer got all yer cups in yer cupboard to be making a racket like that?'

Jap beamed up at him. 'Pork,' he answered, as if that was explanation enough, 'real piggy pork. Schnitzels as big as your turnip, panfuls of grits, pigbellies as huge as a barrage balloon filled with leavings . . .' He paused for breath, eyes glittering feverishly, saliva dripping down his unshaven yellow chin.

Suddenly Ox-Jo understood. The surly look vanished from his face to be replaced by one of suppressed excitement. 'Yer mean – *nobble a porker*?'

Jap had nodded his head, not trusting himself to speak in case that delightful vision of a massive 150-kilo pig roasting on a spit, dripping fat in little splutters into the fire, vanished irretrievably. That was how it had started.

Now as they crept across the dark silent farmyard towards the pig-sty their dream was about to be realized, or so it seemed. Gently, very gently, they pulled back the bolt on the door of the sty and began to open it, keeping their eyes on the farmhouse as the hinges creaked alarmingly. Nothing happened. They peered inside. A huge pig was standing there, hemmed in by the walls so that it couldn't move more than a few millimetres and thereby lose any of the precious weight that had been built up so assiduously all winter by the unknown farmer.

'Shit,' Jap breathed in awe, 'the shit's almost as big as you, Ox!'

'Hold yer water,' Ox-Jo commanded urgently, uncorking the bottle which they had bought on the hamlet's black market with the money they had collected in a whipround of their fellow NCOs. The sty was filled with the sharp fumes of powerful alcohol. The huge pig grunted and craned his massive head with difficulty. Ox-Jo beamed, took one tiny slug of the precious liquid, and held it out to the pig. 'All right, porker, put a belt of that behind yer collar, yer lucky bugger.' Obediently, as it had been trained to do by the farmer, the pig started to drink the *aquavit* like mother's milk.

Fifteen minutes later the great beast was dead drunk and made not a murmur as they loaded it onto one of the farmer's own wheelbarrows. On tip-toes, like characters in a pre-war Theo Ling[1] movie, they started to gently wheel the barrow past the sleeping farmhouse and onto the track that led back into the hamlet where their fellow plotters would already be waiting to dispatch the beast to a porker's heaven; for the whole operation was 'black' and had to be completed before the rest of the HQ was awake. "Cos you know what'll happen if *they* find out,' Jap had warned them before they had left, '*they*'ll be eating schnitzel and the likes of us poor stubble-hoppers'll be lucky if we get a bit of bacon grease to scrape onto our bread.'

But unknown to Jap, this particular May day there would be neither schnitzel nor a scrape of bacon grease passing down into his lean, hungry stomach.

It was when they were halfway down the track, the pig snoring heavily in the barrow, their own breath coming in harsh, hectic gasps under the strain of that tremendous but delicious weight, that they caught their first glimpse of the intruders.

The moon came out momentarily and outlined the shape of the rocks to their right, standing up like the spires of some bizarre, modernistic cathedral. But it wasn't the strangely shaped rocks that made the two men halt in their tracks, the pig forgotten. It was the long file of men plodding along the ridge above them which caught their startled attention, bent like hunchbacks under their packs, their rifles clearly outlined.

Simultaneously and without a word, they both lowered the handles of the barrow and deposited the snoring pig on the ground.

'What do you make of that, apeshit?' Ox-Jo asked in

[1] A well-known German comedian.

an involuntary whisper. 'We didn't put any patrols out tonight, did we?'

Jap shook his head.

Ox-Jo frowned, while the pig snored happily. All the spare men still available at Divisional Headquarters had been pushed out a couple of kilometres into the area around the hamlet. All that remained to defend it was *Stormtroop Edelweiss*, but as General Dietl's HQ was located right in the centre of the divisional area, what need would there be for a patrol? Could it be a patrol from some other outfit? But what would they be patrolling here for, away from the enemy?

'What do you make of it, Jap?' he asked urgently.

By way of an answer, Jap turned his clever little face slightly and sniffed the air.

'Well?' Ox-Jo demanded urgently, counting the men plodding along the skyline and telling himself they couldn't be a patrol, there were too many of them.

Jap frowned and sniffed even harder. 'They're not our people at all events,' he announced after a while. 'We smell of sausage and that shit they call tobacco . . . Those fellers over there, they smell of good soap, not ersatz like that iron-hard stuff we're issued with . . . and Virginia cigarettes . . . *real* cigarettes.' He emphasized the word and looked deliberately at his running-mate.

Ox-Jo knew why. There was only one nation on the whole of the Continent who could afford to issue their soldiers with Virginia cigarettes – real cigarettes. 'Tommies?' he breathed.

Jap nodded his head grimly. 'Tommies,' he echoed.

'But what the shit are they doing here?'

Jap shrugged carelessly. 'Am I Jesus?'

Ox-Jo looked in alarm at the pig snoring happily in the wheelbarrow. 'But the porker,' he protested. 'What about the porker?'

Jap made an impossible suggestion about what Ox-Jo could do with the pig and added hastily, 'We've no time for good grub now, Ox. They're trouble and we want to be out of here before . . .' He stopped short as Ox-Jo bent down to the sleeping, snoring pig. 'Hey, you stupid horned ox, what yer doing?'

'I'M FUCKING WELL KISSING GOODBYE TO MY BREAKFAST, THAT'S WHAT I'M DOING!' Ox-Jo roared in sudden rage, planting a juicy kiss on the porker's wet, happy snout. Then they were gone, slipping silently into the gloom to report what they had just seen.

'Last break,' Ferguson announced and the men slumped happily into the snow, as the pale wintry sun slipped over the edge of the peaks, balanced there for a while, as if considering whether it should stay this day, and then vanished again, as if the effort wouldn't be worth it. 'Professor . . . and you, Sarnt-Major, come with me. We'll go and have a little look-see at what's going on down there.'

Obediently MacDonald followed the major, his rage increasing by the minute. Little look-bleeding-see! His nibs made it all sound like a peacetime scheme at Aldershot.

Below them a large valley opened up with, at its centre, a small hamlet of mainly wooden houses, their roofs heavy with snow, with here and there a thin trail of blue smoke rising from a chimney into the still, grey, dawn air. There was no sign of life, save for what appeared to be a wheelbarrow on the track leading into the place. The sides of the valley were dotted with small tumbledown farms, but even here there was little sign of life, save for the usual dawn cackling and crowing of chickens and cocks.

'All fast asleep,' Ferguson declared.

'So much for German efficiency,' Professor-Doctor Freund said with a smirk. 'In the middle of so-called total war and they are sleeping in as if it were a peacetime Sunday.'

'There are two sentries outside that bigger house in the

middle of the place,' MacDonald said, not even requesting permission to speak.

'Yes, I've already seen them, Sarnt-Major,' Major Ferguson said evenly. 'And you know why they are there? I shall tell you,' he answered his own question before MacDonald had time to do so. 'Because they are guarding the headquarters of the divisional general. They are as good as a signpost for us . . .'

For a time the three men surveyed the hamlet and MacDonald waited for the officers' pronouncements, with growing anger and unease. It all looked too easy to him. He knew old Jerry. He was a cunning bugger. They wouldn't get away with it, whatever the major said; he knew that in his bones.

Finally Major Ferguson announced his intentions. 'Sarnt-Major, I go in with the main party. We'll keep up the pretence that we are followers of this chap Quisling and I am sure the Professor-Doctor here can talk us in close enough to make it almost impossible for the Hun to stop us, once we crack into action. We'll rush the place . . . er, deal with the general and his staff, and then beat a very hasty retreat. Naturally all hell will be let loose and that's where you will come in, Sarnt-Major.'

'Sir,' MacDonald said out of habit, telling himself that both of them, the officer and the Norwegian Yid, were mad; they didn't stand a cat's chance in hell. He thought about his Jocks and frowned.

'You'll hold this ridge here. You can have both brens. Once we start pulling out and the Boche think they've got us on the run, you and your chaps will go into action with all you've got. That'll shake them.' He beamed at the big NCO.

'Yessir. I see, sir,' MacDonald replied woodenly, knowing that nothing would stop the major now. His eyes were full of glory, the DSO, promotion, a battalion of his own. 'When, sir?'

Ferguson looked at his watch. 'Thirty minutes from now.'

'Sir!'

The Professor-Doctor laughed. He laughed easily like a man who had a clear conscience – absolutely sure of himself, had always been so. 'Give me that revolver again, Major,' he said, 'and I'll shoot the famous General Dietl myself.'

Major Ferguson laughed, too, just as easily. 'No, I reserve that pleasure for myself, Professor. I'm a regular soldier. I need the gong. It's good for promotion.'

Inwardly Sergeant-Major MacDonald groaned. He was in the presence of madmen.

## SIX

'British infantry – the best in the world,' Sergeant-Major MacDonald told himself, following the progress of the attack-group with Ferguson's binoculars which the major had left behind. How often as a hard, unsentimental kid from the East End had his heart gone out to them in the Old War when he'd seen them going over the top! More than once they'd been dribbling a football or singing the old songs, the sentimental, crude, obscene ones, that even now twenty-odd years later he could not bear to hear anyone sing; and as the machine guns had begun to chatter and they'd gone in with bayonets, more than one of them had died singing. Now he prayed that Ferguson and the other madman were right and he was wrong and that there would be no slaughter this grey, threatening morning.

His fingers gripping the binoculars wet with sweat and shaky, he observed how the long file of men in their strange uniform, but recognizably Guardsmen all the same, moved ever closer to the hamlet. All the time he kept flashing the glasses from them to the collection of little wooden huts, anxiously. All was apparently silent and at peace, with here and there the smoke curling lazily out of the chimneys, growing a little thicker, as if someone had just woken up and thrown an extra log on the fire or into the stove to warm the night-cold room up a little; and the two grey-uniformed sentries continued their bored pacing up and down the general's quarters, as if the only thing they had on their minds at this moment was a hot drink, a warm-up in front of the guardhouse fire and kip. Everything seemed to be going as Major Ferguson had planned it.

Major Ferguson, nearly half a mile away, did the same

as the worried Sergeant-Major. His keen eyes were everywhere, surveying the ground to his front and then the buildings, watching for the first sign of suspicious movement, the first startled white face at a window, mouth open ready to shout a warning. Once a dog began barking somewhere to their right and Ferguson jumped.

Professor-Doctor Freund smiled in that superior manner of his, which Ferguson was coming to hate, and said calmly, 'Just a dog, my dear Major.'

'I know,' Ferguson snarled. 'Just a little edgy, that's all.'

They went on, each man alone with his thoughts, like a weary farmer plodding home after a hard day's work in the fields, pondering what he had to do on the morrow, brow creased in a frown.

Ferguson threw a glance at the general's hut. The sentries had seen them and the taller one had unslung his rifle, but as far as he could make out at this distance, there was no alarm on the man's face. He was just preparing to challenge them in the time-honoured fashion. Ferguson even knew what he would shout, Freund had told him. It would be '*Wer da?*' Then he would halt the column. Professor-Doctor Freund would go on alone, smiling all the time, hands raised behind the back of his neck, with a grenade clasped in them. For a medical man, Ferguson told himself, he was decidedly bloodthirsty. At fifty feet the good doctor would throw the grenade at the sentries and drop to the ground. That would be the signal. They'd charge the place. With a bit of luck they'd be inside before the Huns woke up to what was happening. Together with Freund, who knew Dietl by sight, they'd dispose of him and any other of his senior officers who were unfortunate enough to be around. With luck it would be all over in five minutes, then they'd be off, covered by MacDonald and his group. In the confusion it would take the Hun an eternity to get organized and by that time they'd be back at the farm owned by Freund's political friend. In spite of his tension, Ferguson smiled. Of course they'd give him a good gong for this and Winston, a friend of his father's, would see it was in all the papers. There'd be a promotion in it, too. But it was not really all that which made him already feel elated; it was the thought that he was demonstrating to those Colonel Blimps back home with their feet up around the fire at their clubs and their eternal damned malt whiskies that this was the way a modern England should fight a war: hard, determined, brutal, with no punches pulled.

'Major,' Freund's voice broke into his excited thoughts.

'Yes?'

Freund smiled at him, perfectly calm, dammit, for a man who had never been in action before. Perhaps as a doctor he knew of some sort of tablet that soothed the nerves? 'I think the psychological moment has come.' He indicated the taller sentry who was bringing his rifle down. 'You say I must count to three after I pull the pin?'

'Yes, I've given the grenade a four minute fuse. Throw it high like a cricket ball – oh, of course, you wouldn't know about cricket. Well throw it and hit the deck at once and don't look up to see what has happened. We'll take care of the rest.'

'Do not fear. I am complete master of my nerves, Major. You see.' He opened his hand, in which he held the grenade, and Ferguson saw he had already pulled out the cotter-pin. All that prevented it from going off now was the pressure of his fingers on the lever. Ferguson was impressed. Even trained soldiers were a bit scared of that kind of trick. Hand grenades were notoriously unreliable things.

'I see,' Ferguson said, as the taller sentry clutched his rifle to his hip, bayonet gleaming and opened his mouth.

'Now I go,' Freund said and started to lift his hands. 'Now he will challenge.'

Freund was wrong. With startling suddenness, the machine gun hissed into life. A line of slugs stitched up frozen snow and Freund leapt back, horror all too apparent on his sallow face. He shouted something in

Norwegian, perhaps a protest, perhaps a cry of alarm. Ferguson never knew, for they were the doctor's last words on this earth. The next burst ripped into his slim, well-manicured hands. The grenade dropped from suddenly bloody and nerveless fingers. Ferguson could hear the 'zing' as the lever flew off and it exploded almost immediately. The earth erupted beneath the doctor. His legs were torn from his body. Suddenly he was a dwarf standing somehow upright for one horrifying moment, watching the red blood pump upwards from his severed legs like some kind of bizarre fountain and then he fell face forward onto the snow. The Guardsmen were shouting and scrambling pell-mell for cover. Everything was abruptly roaring and flashing. Rifles cracked. A mortar thumped. Its bombs came tumbling down. Dirt and rock flew everywhere, and the air was filled with a thick *whooshing* sound, as if someone was swinging round a gigantic broom. Abruptly the ground was trembling and vibrating, as though it, too, had gone mad with fright.

Watching, horrified, on the hill-top, MacDonald cried to himself, 'Ferk it, that's sodding well torn it!' To his young Guardsmen, he said, his voice as steady as rock, 'All right lads, watch it. Get them rifles ready . . .'

Ferguson lay flat on the ground, feeling it rise and fall beneath him as the Germans mortared him and his men. He lay pressed to the earth, as if he was embracing the woman he loved, sexually. All his instincts told him to stay put, not to move. Every fibre of his reason fought against raising himself even a quarter of an inch. His mind commanded him to become part of that earth he hugged so greedily. But he knew that couldn't be. He was an officer – an officer of the Brigade of Guards – and he had to command, take charge, save his men from the mess he had got them into; for he realized instinctively from the volume of fire that the Huns had been well prepared for them. There would be no easy, lightning action now. It was simply and overwhelmingly a matter of saving their skins. He raised his head.

About ten Guardsmen lay sprawled out some ten to twenty yards to his front. He judged them dead by the awkward or extravagant angle at which they lay. There was plenty of blood spread out on the snow, already beginning to harden in the icy dawn air. To left and right, other Guardsmen crouched or lay full-length, rifles still clutched in their hands, their shoulders heaving every time one of the damned mortar bombs came howling out of the sky with that obscene *thump* and hit the ground. The Huns were 'walking' the bombs onto them. In a few minutes they'd be bursting right in the midst of his men. He flung another quick look to left and right, trying to ignore the howl of the bomb splinters cutting the air everywhere. There was a machine gun firing to his right flank and perhaps a light machine gun or automatic rifle or pistol to the left. He ducked as a concentrated volley of fire came from his rear, but not from fear. He could tell from that well-trained slam of fire that it was MacDonald's Guardsmen who were firing. Only the brigade shot like that. In spite of the damnable position he found himself in, he felt a surge of pride run through him. They would be Guardsmen to the very end, come what may. He raised his voice so that they could all hear. 'Now listen carefully! Sergeant-Major MacDonald has got the situation well under control to the rear. He is giving us covering fire. We shall move back in groups. I shall bring up the rear here. Do you all understand? Answer!'

The years of rigid training paid off. Afraid or not, the voices came back from all sides. 'Understood sir . . . understood sir.'

'Excellent. Now the men to my right. Do you hear me? Answer!'

They answered.

'Good. I shall count to three. Then I want you all up and running. There is a slight depression to our immediate rear. Head for that. Once you have reached it, open fire immediately. One . . . two . . . three!'

Ferguson rose to his feet and, standing upright, as if he were back on some peacetime pistol range, one hand behind his back, he began to pump shots to left and right, while his men scrambled back frantically.

'In three devil's' name,' Greul breathed in awe, 'that fellow is either completely mad or damned brave!' Then he forgot the lone English officer standing there, not deigning to notice the mortar bombs which were creeping steadily forward to where he stood. 'Sergeant-Major Meier,' he barked above the thump of the mortar and the rattle of the heavy machine gun, as if someone were running a stick along a length of iron railways, 'the Tommies are trying to do a bunk – and the general wouldn't like it . . . Get a group of the men up to the right and try to stop them. At the double!'

'Let the poor buck-teethed English shits go,' a little voice inside him sneered, 'they ain't got a cat's chance in hell.' But to Major Greul, standing there imperiously, every millimetre a National Socialist officer, right off the cover of a recruiting poster, he barked, '*Jawohl, Herr Major! . . . Zubefehl Herr Major!*'

'*Lick-spittle!*' Jap said scornfully, 'who kisses an officer's arse regularly before breakfast!' And then he, too, was up and running with the rest of them to cut off the poor doomed Tommies.

'Ten o'clock . . . rapid fire!' MacDonald barked, as he saw the group of Germans in their peaked caps rise and start to run double-crouched low, to cut off the first bunch of the retreating Guardsmen. Sweating like a pig, he inserted another magazine and began working his bolt back and forth, pumping bullet after bullet at the running enemy soldiers. Next to him the bren-gunner undid his flies and let loose a rush of hissing yellow urine on the barrel of his bren which glowed a dull purple. Steam rushed into the cold air. Not even taking time to thrust his sexual organ back, he flopped to the snow again and fired a rapid burst at the Germans.

But now they, too, were taking fire from the Germans, as more and more men poured out of the huts, some coming to a sudden stop and collapsing as they were hit, but most of them throwing themselves down into the snow and directing their bullets at the men crouched on the hillside. MacDonald's mind raced. What was he to do? Should he stay there and help to cover what was already a nasty mess, or should he try the old Brigade of Guards' tactic – a sharp sudden, all-out bayonet charge into the enemy's flank to throw him off balance?

Down below Ferguson's left group was pulling out, doubling to the rear, while the right group in position covered them, the slugs beating up the snow in angry white spurts all around their flying heels, with the major not running, but merely walking backwards, firing to left and right like some nineteenth century officer in one of the paintings they had hung in the Guards' Club, gallant and totally cool. And then it happened. Horrified, MacDonald saw how the major staggered as if he had walked into an invisible wall. The revolver dropped from his hand and hung down his side, held there by the lanyard. For one terrible moment, the watching sergeant-major thought he was going to collapse. No! Somehow or other, he pulled himself together. Turning, ignoring the enemy fire altogether, he staggered to where the rest waited, zig-zagging from side to side like a drunken man. A few moments later he had vanished from sight, helped into the depression that was dead ground by the survivors of the German trap; and as he did so, Sergeant-Major MacDonald knew with the sudden certainty of a revelation that the company was finished. Major Ferguson and his Jocks wouldn't get out any more. It was either surrender or fight to the death. He dropped his rifle to the snow and turned on his back to think, though he knew in his innermost self that there wasn't much to think about now; that there was only one decision *he* could take . . .

## SEVEN

Another of the mortar shells slammed into the ground ten yards away. A Guardsman flopped face forward, dead instantly. Another reeled back, his face a myriad of bleeding cuts, as if someone had scrubbed it with a wire pan-cleaner. 'I'm sorry, sir,' he said to Ferguson sitting in the centre of the depression, holding his wounded shoulder, 'but I think that last one did for ma eyes.' He sat down abruptly and began to bleed to death.

'Here they come agen!' someone yelled, as the softening-up barrage stopped and the Germans came rushing out of the choking smoke, bayonets fixed, machine pistols chattering frenetically.

'Get at them, lads!' Ferguson croaked and Guardsman Craig helped him up to the edge of the hole, next to the dead Guardsman. 'Remember we're the Guards!'

As one they opened fire. Germans went down everywhere. A tall man leading the attack took a bullet in the shoulder and went reeling round like a dancer executing a difficult turn. A little German grabbed him before he hit the ground. Still the others came on, shouting furiously, taking casualties all the time. Now they were only yards away. Would nothing stop the bastards? Ferguson asked himself angrily. His teeth gritted in almost unbearable agony, he pulled out his last grenade. Somehow or other he tugged out the cotter pin and let the lever fly off. 'One . . . two . . . three,' he counted off the seconds, as the Germans came ever closer, so that he could see every detail of their dirty, unshaven, sweat-lathered faces, then he flung it.

It exploded in a furious sheet of yellow flame. The leading Germans went reeling back or to the sides, a mass of flailing limbs, their screams of agony drowning even the roar of the explosion. A huge, steaming, brown hole appeared suddenly like the work of some giant mole, filled with dead and dying Germans; and then the rest were rushing back the way they had come, fighting and jostling each other in a frantic attempt to escape that deadly fire, with the tall man who had led the attack struggling after them, supported by the smaller one.

'Cease-fire,' Ferguson cried wearily and tensed as the first obscene thump of the mortar indicated that more of its deadly bombs were on the way. He slumped back to the bottom of the hole and asked himself, how long they would last now?

'Ouch!' Ox-Jo yelped angrily, as Jap ripped open his shirt with his knife, saw the thick red flow, shook his head and began to apply the wound pad which flushed pink almost immediately, 'that hurt!'

'What do yer expect? You've got a shitting big hole in yer flipper. Ah well, it'll mean a medal and another mark a week for yer pension.'

'Yer know what yer can do with yer shitting pension,' Ox-Jo cried above the racket kicked up by the mortar barrage. 'The way this little lot is going on, I don't think many of us'll be around to collect it . . .' He stopped short.

Major Greul was standing there, emerging from the smoke like some Nordic god of old, come down from the fogs of Valhalla to encourage the Viking warriors, engaged in hard, bloody combat. 'Only a scratch, Meier, eh?' he said with one of his wintry smiles.

'It's not so bad, sir,' Ox-Jo heard himself saying, though inside his head a little voice snorted angrily, '*Only a shitting scratch!* Christ, it feels as if my whole shitting arm has fallen off – and then some!'

Greul nodded encouragingly. 'This time when the barrage stops, we'll finish them off. The general himself is going to take a hand. He has organised his HQ staff into an assault group. We'll go in on three sides. I on this flank, Colonel Stuermer on the other, the general will take the centre.' He gave them another wintry smile and moved away back into the smoke, presumably to pass on the good news to the rest of his group.

'What a stupid shit!' Jap growled, finishing bandaging Ox's wound. 'That man's got his head up his arse-permanently!'

'That you can say agen,' Ox-Jo agreed and winced. His arm ached like hell; it was as if some sadistic bastard was stirring around the wound with a red-hot spoon. 'What I wouldn't give for a good slug of sauce!'

'What I wouldn't give for a whole shitting *barrel* of this stuff!' Jap said moodily. 'Norway, I've had it up to here.' His little yellow hand sliced the air underneath his flat nose. 'I've had a noseful, I can tell yer. Let 'em give it back to the shitting penguins.' He spat on the blood-stained snow, littered with the cruel debris of war, in disgust. 'By the Great Whore of Buxtehude and all Her Poxed-Up, Slack-Cunted Daughters, how long is this going to go on!'

It was the same question that Major 'Red Rory' Ferguson was asking himself, as the awesome pounding continued, the warm blood from his wound trickling down still unnoticed. He stared around at his Jocks crouched low in the depression, most of them now wounded like himself. They had all sunk into a strange lethargy. They neither jumped nor trembled now when yet another of the damned mortar bombs slammed home, covering them with dirt and stones. They seemed completely calm, but their eyes, wild, wide and covered with a hot sheen, as if they might break down and sob at any moment, revealed the tremendous strain they were under. Ferguson's heart went out to them suddenly. They were his men, his own people, big, honest, not too bright men, given to drink and whoring, but the best that Scotland could produce.

Abruptly Ferguson realized that in all his long years of service with the brigade, he had never felt much for his soldiers. They had always been there, loyal, obedient, to be dealt with by the NCOs, really. Yet here they were in this God-forsaken hole at the end of the road, loyal to him to the very last, uncomplaining, willing, prepared to die for a hopeless cause. Suddenly the Laird of the Seven Lochs' eyes flooded with tears. He fought them back and, raising his voice over the *thump-thump* of the mortar, said, 'I think . . . we've about . . . had it.'

They looked at him slowly, very slowly, turning their heads, as if they were worked by rusty ancient springs. Their eyes were full of dumb expectancy.

As the barrage started to peter off, indicating that another infantry attack would soon be on its way, Major Ferguson put that overwhelming question that he had thought *he* would never have to pose to them. 'Men, can we surrender? It would mean we would go into the bag for the rest of the war, but we'd live . . .' His voice trailed away. He could already see they were not prepared to do that.

'Permission to speak, sir?' Guardsman Menzies said in his thick coarse Gorbals accent which Ferguson found barely intelligible at times.

Ferguson nodded.

'I say, fuck that for a tale!' Menzies snarled. 'Yon fuckin' Jeries are no a patch on us. Fuck 'em!' Menzies wiped the blood trickling down his tough, mean face away.

Ferguson smiled. 'Well said, Guardsman Menzies. All right, men. In the Old War, my father who commanded this battalion in France, told me the Hun called the Jocks the ladies from hell. Let us show them that even without the kilt we live up to the tradition of our forefathers.' He paused a mere fraction of a second, knowing that when he gave that final command, he would be committing each and every one of the survivors to death; then he said it, 'Fix bayonets!'

With fingers that felt like thick sausages, their movements incredibly slow, they did as he commanded, attaching the long, unwieldy bayonets to the ends of their Lee Enfields.

For one drawn-out moment Major Ferguson remembered that hot summer's day so long ago when he had carried the flag, the blare of the bands, the thump of the big drum, the clip-clop of the horses' hooves, the slap of eight hundred hands shouldering arms with absolute precision – and then they were off slow-marching in front of the old bearded king in perfect formation, the best soldiers in the British Army, the whole world. What a surge of dizzying pride had he felt that day as an eighteen-year old ensign! Now he felt again that same hot, overwhelming pride in this handful of ragged, blood-stained, frozen men. They were the Guards, the Scots Guards. 'Guardsman Menzies,' he cried in a thick full voice, 'give me a hand to get up!'

'Sir!' Menzies barked, as if he were back at Caterham.

He helped Ferguson to his feet. The mortaring had stopped. He could see the peak-capped Germans coming out of the smoke again cautiously, bodies crouched like men advancing against heavy rain. They were coming in for the kill. He straightened up. His voice hard and firm, his wound forgotten, he cried, 'B Company, Second Battalion Scots Guards – will advance . . . NOW!'

Supported by the broken rifle he was using as a crutch he started to hobble forward to meet the enemy, followed by the survivors, swaying like drunks.

'Scotland the brave . . . Scotland for ever!' Menzies croaked.

'Scotland for ever!' the others took up the cry.

Above on the ridge MacDonald heard that last hoarse cry, as they disappeared into the smoke below for good, and knew he would never see any one of them again. Unable to speak, he jerked his thumb over his shoulder. He rose. Wordlessly his men did the same. Shoulders bent in defeat, trailing their rifles in the snow, they disappeared into the pines.

'*Scotland for ever!*' the cry seemed to go on and on . . .

'Don't shoot . . . for God's sake don't shoot!' Colonel Stuermer bellowed to Greul's group as the English came reeling out of the smoke like sleepwalkers, his face full of awed respect for these filthy apparitions who were dead on their feet, hardly able to carry their long bayonets. 'Take their weapons off—' He stopped short, his voice trailing away into nothing, as the enemy broke into a shambling trot, with, at their head, an officer hobbling along, his red hair gleaming in the first rays of the sun breaking through the smoke.

Major Greul heard that desperate cry, but he took no notice of it. A smile of cruel satisfaction on his lean face, he raised his machine pistol. Standing there, legs spread slightly, machine pistol clutched to his hip, he seemed all-powerful, a veritable symbol of the new Germany, freed from the soft decadence and weakness of the old Continent. He pressed his trigger and felt the powerful, almost sexual throbbing of the mp at his hip. '*FIRE AT WILL!*' he cried.

'*NO!*' Colonel Stuermer yelled desperately, but his voice was already drowned by that tremendous final volley . . .

# *ENVOI*

*'Wer mit dem Teufel isst braucht einen langen Loeffel.'*

*Old German Saying*[1]

[1] He who eats with the Devil needs a long spoon.

Down below in Narvik the funeral pyres of thick black smoke rose stiffly into the grey evening sky. They burned everywhere. Out at sea, the transports waited, as more and more of the little launches chugged out to them, white water curving in hard Vs from their sterns. The heavy silence down there was broken at regular intervals as the English sappers blew up yet another ammunition dump. Occasionally a Messerschmitt came barrelling in at 400mph, machine guns chattering, sending white and red tracer racing towards the long lines of men in khaki waiting to embark in the launches. Flak filled the air with cottonballs of grey smoke, but the men down below did not even look up. They were too weary, too downtrodden. They had fought the Germans for two months – and almost beat them. Now with the Germans sweeping through France and getting ever closer to the Channel Ports, with the British Army in that country reeling before them, they were being recalled to help the best they could. Britain needed every last man in France this terrible June of 1940.

General Dietl, standing on the edge of the division's perimeter high above the port, lowered his glasses and said, a note of satisfaction in his voice which did not altogether hide his weariness, 'Well, gentlemen, they are going at last.'

'Yessir,' Greul rasped, eyes gleaming with triumph, 'we've beaten them. Narvik will be ours before the night's out!'

Dietl nodded and there was a murmur of agreement from his officers. 'Yes, I have already signalled the Führer that we will re-occupy Narvik at twenty-four hundred hours this day.' He frowned and then smiled again. 'It was quite an amateurish operation really, gentlemen. The English should have won the day, but thanks to you, my dear Stuermer,' he looked at Colonel Stuermer, still pale and shaky from the time he had spent in the primitive divisional hospital after he had been wounded for the second time, 'we managed to pull if off.'

'Thank you, sir,' Stuermer answered dutifully, though he felt no pride, just weariness. Victory always meant death and dishonour for the other side; it was too high a price to pay.

'There the last of them go, sir,' Dietl's excited young aide reported.

As one, the officers focused their glasses. The men waiting on the beach had gone. The launches were now chugging out to the transports. Smoke was beginning to pour thickly from their stacks. They could hear the rattle of anchor chains being raised quite distinctly. A Messerschmitt came roaring in, but no flak answered the first preliminary burst of machine gun fire, and the pilot gave up. There were no more easy targets available on the beach. He gave a triumphant victory roll and winged away to the east.

Now the sun was beginning to set, slipping into the dark green sea and flushing the crags of the mountains a deep pink. Long black shadows were slipping along the fiord and towards the port, as if in a hurry to conceal the price of failure.

'Alert the advance party, Lieutenant,' Dietl commanded his excited young aide, who had not taken part in the fighting; he had been flown in later and was fresh and green, and very keen.

'Yessir!' The aide doubled away, as if he had been ordered to make a single-handed attack on London itself.

The soft sad wail of the bagpipes came from one of the transports slowly beginning to move out of the fiord towards the open sea and England. It sent a frisson of sadness and failure down Stuermer's spine. He could feel the small hairs stand erect at the back of his head at the strange eerie sound.

'What is the matter, sir?' Greul asked, taking his delighted eyes off the scene below.

'Nothing,' Stuermer answered. 'A louse must have run over my liver or something.' He took one last look at Narvik and the departing English, then snapped, 'Get the men together, Greul. Soon *Stormtroop Edelweiss* will have to march again.'

'Why sir?' Greul asked, a little surprised.

Stuermer did not answer. How could he tell the tall, arrogant major in this moment of triumph what was going on in his mind: the overwhelming knowledge that they would be back? That was for certain – *one day the English would return . . .*

**FIRE OVER KABUL**
**Stormtroop 6**

**LEO KESSLER**

1942: 'GENTLEMEN, I WILL NOW TELL YOU HOW WE WILL CRUSH THE ENGLISH!'

And so, Colonel Stuermer, C.O. of Germany's elite reconnaissance and assault company, Edelweiss, learns of their next mission. At *Reichsführer* Himmler's command, Stormtroop Edelweiss are to travel over treacherous terrain in hostile lands to make the inaccessible, accessible. Pioneering a route from Kabul in neutral Afghanistan, through impenetrable mountains in Nepal, dank rain forests in Assam, Stuermer and his men will herald the liberation of India. For the Germans – using Edelweiss's matchless skills – and their Jap allies have promised the Indian people their freedom . . .

FUTURA PUBLICATIONS
FICTION/WAR
0 7088 2223 1

**WAVE OF TERROR**
**Stormtroop 7**

**LEO KESSLER**

Colonel Stuermer's valiant, intrepid troops are ordered on an impossible mission – to prevent the destruction of the Third Reich!

In August 1943 a roaring armada of American bombers flew in low over the peaceful lush Rumanian countryside. Their mission – to destroy the source of the Führer's power, the mighty petrol refineries at Ploesti. Victory was certain . . . or was it?

For the Germans had been alerted – and they were waiting for them. Stormtroop Edelweiss's daring, suicidal mission to sabotage the enemy planes lying deep in the Libyan desert had paid off – but at what cost?

FUTURA PUBLICATIONS
FICTION /WAR
0 7088 2291 6

**HIMMLER'S GOLD**
**Stormtroop 5**

**LEO KESSLER**

BLOOD MONEY . . .

1944. The Allied stranglehold on Hitler's Germany tightens amid the flames. But in Himmler's mind, the dream of a thousand-year Reich lives on . . .

Dedicated to continuing the Führer's battle, he needs to transport a fortune in diamonds to South America. He needs an elite team, hardened in the most merciless arenas of conflict, to carry them across a Europe rent by war. He needs Stormtroop Edelweiss.

Until Stuermer's men, the dirtiest dozen of them all, begin to make a few plans of their own . . .

FUTURA PUBLICATIONS
FICTION/WAR
0 7088 1843 9